SIXTY MILES TO GLORY

Working for Bellington's Detective Agency wasn't always easy. This Zachary Cobb discovered when he agreed to bring Heather Watkins back to the town of Glory, where she was wanted in connection with the shooting of a prominent businessman. A stagecoach robbery, a second prisoner and being stranded in the desert complicated matters. And what did the four ruthless killers on the trail want? When the killers eventually caught up with them, Cobb found that he was in more trouble than ever.

SIXTY MILES TO GLORY

SIXTY MILES TO GLORY

by
Steven Gray

Dales Large Print Books
Long Preston, North Yorkshire, England.

British Library Cataloguing in Publication Data.

Gray, Steven
    Sixty miles to Glory.

    A catalogue record for this book is
    available from the British Library

    ISBN 1-85389-617-9 pbk

First published in Great Britain by Robert Hale Limited., 1995

Published in Large Print April, 1996 by arrangement with Robert Hale Limited.

Dales Large Print is an imprint of
Library Magna Books Ltd.
Printed and bound in Great Britain by
T.J. Press (Padstow) Ltd., Cornwall, PL28 8RW.

ONE

Zachary Cobb stuffed his dirty shirt, into the saddle-bag and somehow managed to do up the strap. He looked round the hotel bedroom. That was everything. Nothing left behind. Good. Now all he had to do was to go and see Marshal Hepworth and make arrangements about the reward. Then he could be on his way home. To St Louis and civilization. To a well-earned rest.

This was his third job for Bellington's Detective Agency in as many months, all of which had involved going up against dangerous outlaws with nothing to lose if they happened to shoot and kill a private detective. It would be extremely pleasant to have a few weeks' holiday—getting up late, going to the theatre, squiring a young lady around; all without the fear of someone creeping up behind him and shooting him in the back.

Cobb was twenty-nine and, as befitted an employee of Mr Bellington, was always as neat and clean as the circumstances permitted. He had dark-brown hair, cut short, and was clean-shaven. Steely-brown eyes with small lines creasing at their corners provided little clue as to what he was thinking. Tall and lithe, he gave the impression of wiry strength. Dress had to be sombre and tidy and he mostly wore dark colours.

He liked his job and knew he was good at it but, after several months trailing outlaws in Arizona and New Mexico, he felt ready for a rest.

Dawn had only just given way to the pale light of morning. But he was anxious to get his business done, have breakfast and be in good time for the eastbound stage. This early no one was about in Glory's streets as he walked the short distance from hotel to marshal's office.

'I'm all ready to go,' Cobb said, sitting down opposite Oliver Hepworth and accepting a cup of coffee. 'Just want to give you the address of the bank in St

Louis where you can send the reward.'

Bellington's detectives were not allowed to keep the rewards on any wanted criminals they caught; the money had to be paid into the agency's coffers. As paying a poor wage was not among Mr Bellington's many other faults, none of his detectives minded too much, and rarely tried to break a rule which meant instant dismissal if found out.

'OK. I'm glad everything worked out,' Hepworth said. 'Been a pleasure.'

Cobb smiled, nodding his head in acknowledgement. Being a private detective, he knew that his presence was often resented by the local law. They saw his being hired as a slur on their ability and didn't like outside interference in how they did their jobs. Hepworth had proved different. Partly because a while ago he had fallen off his horse, and now had a bad leg, bad back and bad head. He'd been glad of Cobb's help in rounding up a gang of horsethieves who'd roamed the area for some while.

'I'll be on my way then.' Cobb finished

the coffee and stood up.

'Marshal! Marshal!' The cry was echoed by loud footsteps on the wooden sidewalk, coming ever closer.

'Oh, oh,' Hepworth sighed, recognizing trouble when he heard it. 'Now what?'

The door to the office crashed open and his deputy rushed in, face red with exertion and excitement.

'What is it?'

'Marshal!' Tommy Reynolds panted, then taking a gulp and a deep breath, managed to go on. 'There's been a murder!'

'A murder?' Hepworth repeated, glancing at Cobb. Violence was no stranger to the streets of Glory: fist fights, gun duels as well as a number of lesser crimes were common occurrences. But murder, that was something else. 'You sure you ain't mistaken?'

'No, Marshal. You'd better come and see.'

Reluctantly Hepworth eased himself out of the chair, suppressing a twinge of pain. He considered it foolish to be suffering so much agony from a simple fall but the doc had said he'd landed awkwardly and part of the trouble was that none of them was getting any younger. He'd been told to rest but that wasn't easy, and if Tommy was right, a murder would surely make it impossible.

'Will you come with us, Mr Cobb?'

With a sinking feeling that he was going to regret this, Cobb nodded. Every instinct told him to head for the hotel and the stagecoach; every instinct except two—curiosity and the ingrained teachings of Mr Bellington which said no crime should go unpunished.

'It's this way, down by the creek,' Tommy said, leading the way.

That was where the small but thriving redlight district was situated.

'In one of the brothels?' Hepworth asked, thinking that maybe, after all, the murder would be about jealousy, drink or a violent lover, and so easily solved.

'Not exactly.'

Glory's tenderloin area was as deserted as the rest of the streets, except for a

11

couple of cowboys heading home after a night of satisfactory sin, if their tired smiles were anything to go by. Beyond the saloons and brothels, a short roadway led down to the creek. It was lined by several houses and the cribs belonging to those prostitutes who worked for themselves or were set up as mistresses by the town's few prominent businessmen.

Halfway down, a number of people had gathered outside a single-storey house. They all turned to watch and, as the lawmen approached, their excited babbling gradually died away.

'Heather Watkins's place,' Hepworth said to Cobb. 'A young prostitute who's not frequent with her favours.' He was rather sorry that something had happened to Heather. She was a pretty young woman with a friendly personality. But whores ran all sorts of risk from all sorts of people.

'We heard a shot in the night.' Mona, a girl who lived nearby, stepped forward. 'Didn't we, Joe?' she nudged the tall man next to her.

'Yeah, Marshal.' Joe looked a bit

sheepish at being caught up in such a situation.

Which well he might, Hepworth decided, seeing as how he was a respectably married man with five children.

'We didn't take any notice,' Mona went on. 'There're always gunshots around here. But then this morning as Joe was leaving I noticed that Heather's windows were closed. In the summer she always sleeps with them open. I was worried because she hadn't told me she wouldn't be at home, which she usually does. So I got Joe to look in.'

'And I saw the body. And went to find Mr Reynolds, who is usually patrolling around here at this time of day.'

No one mentioned that that wasn't because of duty but because the deputy mostly spent his nights in saloon or brothel.

'This way, Marshal,' Tommy said. 'Out of the way, out of the way,' he added to the crowd, acting very proud and important at having been the first lawman on the scene.

Cobb followed Hepworth up on to the porch and peered through the window. He saw a small bedroom, crammed full of furniture and dominated by a bed with a lacy spread hanging to the floor over lacy white sheets and pillowcases. More frilly lace covered dressing-table and a chair.

The look of pretty femininity was spoilt by the body. It lay face up on the bed.

'My God!' Hepworth exclaimed in surprise. 'That's Norman Tomlin!'

'Exactly, Marshal,' Mona said. 'He's a real stranger. I don't remember him ever calling on Heather. From what she said he didn't like whores generally and her particularly. So why is he in there, lying on her bed, shot to death?'

'Tommy, clear these people away.' Hepworth felt this was going to be difficult enough without an audience. 'Have you been inside?'

'No, Marshal, the door is locked.'

Cobb solved this problem easily enough by slamming himself against the door. The flimsy wood around the lock splintered and they found themselves in a parlour which,

14

besides a tiny kitchen at the rear, was the house's only other room.

'Who's this Norman Tomlin?'

'He owns and runs the general store on the corner of Main Street. Or used to,' Hepworth replied as the two men entered the bedroom and stared down at the body on the bed.

The dead man had been in his early fifties and well dressed in dark suit and white shirt. Now there was a large hole in his chest and his arms were flung out from his sides, a look of shocked fear on his face.

'He was extremely well-off and had a number of other business interests.'

'And he didn't frequent the redlight district?'

'Not as far as I knew. He was a member of the church and disapproved of drink, gambling and bad women. It's a real puzzle. I can't think of any reason why Tomlin would visit Heather nor for her to shoot him.'

Cobb shrugged. 'Many a man has secrets. He was here for something and

15

I doubt it was a prayer meeting.'

'Hmm, you're right.'

Cobb was surprised that Norman Tomlin had been able to keep his activities a secret but he wasn't surprised that he had such secret activities. 'Maybe he'd been fooling around with Heather Watkins for some while or maybe he had always fancied her and tried not to give into his feelings seeing them as sinful. Then when he had succumbed, became violent, seeing her as the cause of his fall from grace. Or perhaps he was mean and there was some sort of argument over payment. Whatever happened he's now dead. Shot by the girl.'

Hepworth looked up from where he was going through the pockets of the suit jacket which was lying flung over the chair in the corner. 'I can't believe Heather would do something like that. She's a nice girl, never been in any sort of trouble.' He came back to the bed, stared at Cobb and sighed heavily. 'But maybe you're right. She's taken some clothes with her by the looks of things. And that's not all. It seems she also took the opportunity to rob Tomlin. I can't find his wallet.'

'Would he have come here with a lot of money?'

'Tomlin went most everywhere with a lot of money.'

'So perhaps she simply saw the opportunity to get rich without much effort and took it.'

'It's hard to believe.'

'Whores, even nice ones, usually only think of two things: one's themselves, the other's money. Whatever the truth, whether it was self-defence against a suddenly violent lover or murder done out of greed, there seems little doubt that Heather Watkins shot him. You'll have to bring her in for questioning.'

'I know. The trouble is Tomlin was an important man in Glory. He was on the town council and his fellow members will expect results and quickly. And the way I feel that might not be too easy.' Hepworth sunk down on the bed beside the corpse, face suddenly grey with pain.

'What about your deputy?'

17

'Tommy's a good lad and eager to please but he's none too bright and I daren't trust him with something like this.'

He looked hopefully at Cobb.

Cobb's sinking feeling came back. He knew where this was heading. He didn't want to get involved. He wanted to go back to St Louis. But he also knew what Mr Bellington would expect.

'All right,' he said with a sigh. 'I'll see what I can find out.'

His only consolation was that it seemed like a straightforward case and he couldn't see how there would be any complications.

TWO

Marshal Hepworth went back to his office to sit down and ease his aching back, leaving Cobb to start looking for Heather Watkins with the help of Tommy Reynolds. Tommy was a young man, tall and gangly, with clothes that never seemed to fit properly and a prominent Adam's apple. He reminded Cobb a bit of a puppy. Cobb usually liked to work alone but he knew that, however limited a lawman Reynolds might be, without him the townspeople would be reluctant to speak to a private detective from St Louis, believing that what happened in Glory was none of an outsider's business.

While they waited for the doctor and undertaker whom Hepworth said he would summon, Cobb questioned the few remaining onlookers about the shot. While the respectably married Joe wanted to be on his way home, Mona was only too willing to talk to him.

'The shot came at about two o'clock,' she said. 'But shots ain't unusual around here, although this time it did sound closer than normal. Any shooting usually takes place around the saloons.'

'And you didn't hear anything else, either before or after? No sounds of an argument or a fight, or anyone riding away?'

'People are riding up and down all

19

the time, honey. Besides we were busy.' Giggling, Mona squeezed Joe's arm and cuddled up to him, making him go red and squirm uncomfortably, especially when both Cobb and Tommy grinned.

'And Tomlin had never visited Heather before?' Cobb thought that while Marshal Hepworth might well not know the truth about all of Glory's citizens, a whore would know what went on in her territory.

But all Mona did was frown. 'That's the puzzling thing, honey. Like I told the marshal, Mr Tomlin didn't approve of whores. As far as I know he didn't ever visit anyone down here. He wasn't that sort. Anyway Heather wasn't a whore. She has a regular boyfriend.'

'Who's that?'

'Robin Bartlett,' Tommy replied. 'Owns a ranch just outside of town.'

'And he's the jealous type. She wouldn't want to cheat on him and he wouldn't let her.'

'Maybe he caught them together and shot Tomlin?'

'Doubt it, honey. Usually Heather goes

out to the ranch to see Robin. But if he came into town he stayed all night with her, and he'd join her before two in the morning, wouldn't he? Besides even if he was interested, Mr Tomlin would know Heather was off limits.'

'How come?'

'He and Mr Bartlett were partners,' Tommy said. 'They have been for a couple of years now.'

'Can I go now?' respectably married Joe, wailed. 'My wife's expecting me.'

'Yeah, OK.'

Mona pinched the man's arm. 'See you next week, sweetheart.' And Joe went off followed by grins and comments.

'Did anyone else see anything suspicious last night? Hear anything?'

The rest of the onlookers shook their heads.

'Well if you do remember anything tell the marshal or Deputy Reynolds here.'

As Cobb and Tommy walked away, the deputy said, 'Why all the questions? It seems clear to me that Heather shot Mr Tomlin and then ran away with his money.

21

What other explanation can there be?'

'I agree. But sometimes matters aren't as they obviously seem. It's best to ask questions now rather than jump to conclusions that are later proved wrong.'

Tommy digested this piece of advice, then said, 'What are we going to do now?'

'See if we can find Miss Watkins. If she's not still around town where would she have gone and how?'

'Well.' Tommy began to think, obviously a not terribly easy process for him. 'The stage, either east or west, won't be leaving for a while yet. She could be waiting for either, but I suppose that would be a bit foolish. She'd hardly walk. But she owns her own mare and could have ridden away in any direction.' Tommy might be a bit simple but he clearly knew a lot about the inhabitants of the redlight district.

'Right. Let's go to the livery. The stage office is on the way. We'd better look in there, just in case she is extremely foolish.' And Cobb thought he could ask for a rebate on the stagecoach ticket he wouldn't now be using.

The stagecoach clerk had seen no sign of Heather Watkins.

'But I'll keep an eye open for her in case she tries to get on at the last minute without a ticket.' He spoke as if this was a greater sin than the fact that she had shot someone.

By now the news of what had happened had spread through the town. Men and women gathered excitedly on corners or in the stores gossiping and saying how terrible it all was. Their eyes followed Cobb and Reynolds.

At the livery, the owner, a wizened little man with a bent back, came out to them.

'Have you seen Heather Watkins?' Tommy asked.

The man chewed furiously on his tobacco. 'Her horse ain't here. Last I seen of both was when Heather went out yesterday morning. Going to see that boyfriend of hers she was.' He winked. 'Naughty little gal.'

'What time did she get back?' Cobb said.

'She didn't. Well, at least what I mean is, she hadn't returned by the time I went home. Come to think of it, she was always late back from the ranch.' Again he winked.

'Would there be any way for you to tell if she had got back, seen to the mare and then ridden out again during the night?'

The old man shook his head. 'Livery's open day and night. I ain't here, people help themselves to feed for their horses. No way to know who's done that or when. All I can say for sure is that the mare weren't here this morning when I arrived for work.'

'Did that surprise you?'

'Not really. Heather rarely stays out all night but it has happened. Nice little gal she is for all she's a whore. Always polite and thoughtful. Hope nothing's happened to her.'

'OK. Thanks for your help. Come on, Tommy.'

'Where to now?'

'I think you and me had better go out see this Robin Bartlett. Make sure that

24

Miss Watkins did get back to town last night after all.'

The Circle B Ranch was situated some two hours' ride out of Glory. It was late morning when Cobb and Reynolds approached it, and it was hot, even up here in the foothills where forests of pine trees encroached on all sides and provided welcome shade.

'Mr Bartlett has been here for several years now,' Tommy explained as they approached the ranch buildings. 'He came from somewhere in New Mexico. Doing quite well, although the marshal says he could do better if he really tried. He's a bachelor.'

Which probably explained the rough and ready air about the place. A timber-built house, two storeys high, and looking new and raw, stood alone part way up a rise. The porch was only half completed. Below stood what was the original house, now used as a bunkhouse, a barn and a couple of corrals. Firewood was stacked all along the side of the barn and equipment of various kinds was strewn untidily across the yard.

Some men were watching another cowboy breaking horses. Seeing Cobb and Reynolds, two of the men detached themselves from the others and strolled over.

'Robin Bartlett, that's the good-looking one, and Dean Morrow, his foreman,' Tommy whispered out of the side of his mouth.

Bartlett looked to be in his early thirties. He had wavy blond hair and a small blond beard. His eyes were wide and brown. The man beside him was about the same age but much shorter, although broad with well-muscled arms and shoulders. He was unshaven and where his hat was pushed to the back of his head, Cobb could see that his black hair was untidy and balding in the front.

'Deputy,' Bartlett said as Cobb and Reynolds came to a halt. He eyed Cobb curiously.

'Mr Bartlett, this is Zachary Cobb. He's a Bellington's private detective.'

'Oh?' Bartlett reached up to shake hands.

'But it's not in that capacity I'm here. I'm acting for Marshal Hepworth.'

'Has something happened?'

'Yes. We need to speak to you.'

'You'd better come in then. Have some lemonade and get out of this sun.'

In silence the four men walked up the slope and went into the house. Inside it had just as unfinished a look as outside: the timber for walls and floor was roughly hewn, nothing covered the floors except for a couple of rugs, and the furniture was old and lumpy.

They went into a room stretching all along the front where a window looked down towards the work buildings.

While Bartlett indicated for them to sit down, Morrow fetched in glasses of cold lemonade.

'Now, Mr Cobb is it, what can I do for you?'

'It's about your partner, Norman Tomlin. I'm afraid he's dead.'

'Dead!' Bartlett exclaimed sitting up straight. 'But he can't be. I mean I only saw him yesterday. He was out here at the ranch discussing business. He was all right then. What happened? Did he have an accident?'

'He was shot.'

'Shot!' Bartlett looked at Morrow. 'Shot! Christ, this is awful. How did it happen?'

'We're not exactly sure,' Cobb replied. 'But it seems there was some sort of quarrel with a prostitute, who has now disappeared.'

Morrow laughed. 'That can't be right. Tomlin was never involved with any of the whores. He was an upstanding churchgoer.'

'Nevertheless he was found this morning shot dead in a whore's bedroom.'

Bartlett gulped down half of his lemonade. 'There must be some mistake. Or at least some good reason for him going there. Perhaps he was trying to reform her.'

'At two o'clock in the morning?'

'Well, no, I suppose that doesn't seem likely.'

'Was Heather Watkins also out here yesterday?'

'Yeah, she was,' Bartlett said and then

28

gaped at Cobb. 'My God, you don't mean she was the whore you're talking about?'

'It was her house where Tomlin was found.'

'I don't believe it!' Bartlett jumped to his feet and began pacing up and down. 'She would never cheat on me, especially with Norman! And Norman would never cheat on me either.'

'What time did they leave here?'

Norman left early afternoon, oh, just gone two I guess. Heather stayed on and went back a couple of hours later.'

'On her own?'

'Yeah. I said I'd get one of the men to go with her but they were all out at the time and she was anxious to hurry back for some reason. My God! Don't tell me it was because she had an appointment with Norman!'

'Do you know if Tomlin had a lot of money with him?'

'A fair bit I suppose.'

'Enough to tempt a whore?'

Bartlett moaned. 'Yeah. A couple of hundred dollars at least because he'd been to the bank earlier for money for expenses. Are you saying Heather stole his money?'

'His wallet was missing.'

'But what possible reason could she have for stealing from him?'

Cobb could think of several reasons: escape from a jealous lover, escape from Glory where everyone knew what she was; just escape. While $200 wasn't a fortune, it might well have been enough, with what else she'd managed to save, to tip the balance between staying or going.

'I always gave her plenty of money.'

'Not many whores don't want more,' Morrow put in.

'But Heather's not like that.' Bartlett sat down again and ran a hand through his hair. 'Or at least I didn't think she was.'

'You never thought Norman went with whores,' Morrow reminded him.

'And Heather's disappeared, you say?'

'Yes.'

'And you're trying to find her?'

'For Marshal Hepworth, yes. She's not around town, her horse has gone and she seems to have taken some clothes with her too. There doesn't seem to be any mistake about her guilt.'

'Well I want to be kept informed of what happens. I want to know why Heather and my partner were cheating on me behind my back, and I want to know why she shot him. It must have been her fault. She must have tempted him into it. Norman wasn't just a partner, he was a good friend.'

Evidently Bartlett had conveniently forgotten that Heather wasn't just a whore, she'd been his mistress.

'Tell Marshal Hepworth that I'll be in town tomorrow and if she hasn't been found I'll post a substantial reward for her arrest.'

He stood up to indicate that the meeting was over, and Cobb, unable to think of anything more useful he could ask, also got up.

'She hasn't been found, I suppose?' Cobb said when he and Reynolds reported back to the marshal.

Hepworth shook his head. 'No, I've got around asking questions and I'm sure she ain't in Glory. I've had a dreadful day. It seems like everyone's been here at one time or another demanding that I do something. The town council wants the saloons and brothels closed down. The pimps and madams want to ensure they stay open.'

'I hope they ain't shut,' Tommy said, a bit mournfully.

'Don't worry, son. They bring in too much money for that to happen. The town council might be full of righteous indignation right now but they'll soon come to their senses when they realize that to shut the redlight district will hit them in their pockets where it really hurts. Now, Tommy, will you do me a favour?'

'Sure, Marshal.'

'I want you to go and send a telegraph to the marshals of all the towns around here. Give them Heather's name and description and what we think she's done. Oh, and you'd better add that a reward is going to be offered.'

As Reynolds hurried out, Cobb said, 'Think that'll do any good?'

Hepworth shrugged. 'Mebbe. Even if she had got money on her, Heather is alone, presumably on horseback, and unless this was planned, which I doubt, without much with her. She'll have to stop in a town, sooner or later, to buy supplies, or to pick up a stage. Gal like her ain't easy to miss. Anyway, it's about the only hope there is because she could have gone in any direction and be anywhere by now.'

THREE

Heather Watkins felt that Copper City, which was only sixty miles from Glory, wasn't far enough away for safety.

She'd arrived there two days ago after her flight from the killing of Norman Tomlin. During her ride through the foothills, with no idea of where to go, mind in a turmoil, she'd thought about Copper City. And come to the conclusion that that was where she would head.

For a start, she knew where it was. And it was a reasonably easy and safe journey. Anywhere else might mean crossing mountains or deserts; even heading into Apache country. For another, it was a wild and rough town, a hang-out for drunks and whores who didn't have much time for the law. And, most important, she knew a girl who worked in Batty's Saloon: Christine would provide shelter for a while, until she got her thoughts together.

But Heather knew as soon as she arrived that she couldn't stay long, for Christine hadn't been very pleased to see her and hadn't wanted to get on the wrong side of the law. Christine had met a young store clerk, who worked in Glory, and was hoping to marry him. It was proving difficult enough to convince his family that, despite working in a saloon, she was a decent young woman; being accused of harbouring a whore wanted for murder was hardly likely to help her cause.

'Just for a few days,' Heather pleaded. 'Until I'm safe and the search for me has died down.'

34

'All right,' Christine agreed reluctantly. 'I just don't want any trouble that's all.'

'Neither do I. And can I borrow some of your clothes? These are so dirty.' Heather indicated her travel-stained divided skirt and jacket. 'We're much the same size.'

'Yes, all right. Help yourself.' Christine paused, then said, 'Where will you go after you leave here?'

'I don't know. Away from Arizona that's for sure. I fancy somewhere civilized for a change. Somewhere not full of jealous ranchers and their business partners. San Francisco perhaps. I've always wanted to see the ocean.'

Although she was scared of leaving, maybe tomorrow she would move on, rather than outstay her welcome. She was also scared of staying. What would become of her if she was found, returned to Glory?

Unlike Heather, Christine had never earned a living as a prostitute, she helped serve drinks and ran the roulette wheel, so there was no danger of her bringing men back to her room. But, naturally,

35

she did have a living to earn so Heather stayed in the room alone, listening to the noise below: the talk, the occasional shout, laughter, the honky-tonk piano belting out lively tunes. Unused to inactivity, Heather didn't like being stuck in one room, with nothing to do but think and worry, she wanted to be amongst the light and laughter downstairs,where she would feel more at home.

Footsteps sounded in the corridor outside. Heather took no notice. Most of the other girls weren't as lucky as Christine, they had to entertain the customers, and there was a constant toing and froing.

She was lying back on the bed, twisting at the top button on her blouse, when the door suddenly crashed open, kicked back against the wall.

Heather screamed and jerked upright.

'Hold it right there, missy. Don't try anything!'

Through frightened eyes, Heather saw an old, disreputable-looking man standing in the doorway. He wore a badge and there was nothing old or disreputable about the gun he had pointed at her.

Heart beating wildly, Heather cried out, 'Don't shoot!'

'Just get up slowly and carefully.'

Heather did as she was told, holding her arms slightly away from her body.

The marshal came over, patting her body down searching for hidden weapons. Finding none, he said, 'Are you going to come quietly along with me or do I have to handcuff you?'

With the man's gun stuck in her back, Heather didn't feel she could argue with him.

'Is there anything you want to take with you?'

'No.'

'Right then, let's get you over to the jail and safely locked up.'

He caught hold of her arm and marched her out into the corridor. Several of the girls and the men they were entertaining had come out to look. There were tears of humiliation and fear in Heather's eyes but she straightened her back, not wanting anyone to know how scared she was.

'How did you find me?' she asked as they started down the stairs.

'How do you think?'

Heather glanced over at her supposed friend, who was at the roulette wheel and who refused to look up, even though everyone around her was staring at the marshal and his pretty prisoner.

'There's a reward out on you.'

'Greedy bitch,' Heather mumbled, but all the same she couldn't blame Christine too much. Money might help her marriage prospects.

'Zac, there's a telegraph come through from Marshal Newborn over at Copper City. He's arrested Heather Watkins. Wants to know what we want to do. I suppose someone'll have to pick her up and bring her back.' Hepworth sighed. 'I wish I could go but my back's still playing me up. I couldn't ride all that way. And while Tommy could manage something like that, I need him here with me looking after things.'

'How far is it?'

'Only some sixty miles. And there's a daily stage service.'

'All right,' Cobb said disagreeably. 'I'll go.'

'You can ride there and get the stage back. Shouldn't take long. Two days, three at the most. I'll send a message to Robin Bartlett telling him.'

'I'd rather you didn't.'

'Oh, why?'

'Well for a start, this girl who's been arrested might not be Heather Watkins. Newborn could have made a mistake. And for another, I'm not too fond of the thought that maybe Bartlett will take it into his head to want to handle this himself. He looked the type who might. So did some of his men.'

Bartlett had been in Glory the day before for Norman Tomlin's funeral. He'd made a lot of noise about the inadequacy of the local law not yet catching Tomlin's killer, and last night before he and his crew had gone back to the Circle B, a lot of drink had been consumed in various saloons, accompanied by a lot of ugly talk.

'They never actually do anything wrong that I can charge 'em with but the high jinks of both Bartlett and some of his men do threaten to get out of hand now and then. However, that's a lot different to doing anything about Heather, even if he is angry about her betrayal and Tomlin's death. But you're mebbe right. There have been rumours about Bartlett taking the law into his own hands in the past, and several rustlers who strayed on to his land haven't been seen again.

'I'll wait until you've confirmed it is Heather and then I'll make sure he understands you won't tolerate any interference.'

'Good.'

'And, Zac, thanks for this.'

Cobb nodded. He wasn't any too pleased. He felt that acting as escort for a prostitute, even one accused of murder, was beneath his dignity. Still if Hepworth was right and all he had to do was stay at Copper City one night and then deliver the prisoner back to Glory, it didn't sound any too difficult and certainly not dangerous.

And, once she was safely ensconced in Glory's jail, maybe, at last, he could go back to St Louis and civilization.

Hepworth detailed a way through the foothills which he said was quicker than following the stage road, which went the longer but easier way by crossing the flat desert. Wanting to get to Copper City in one day, Cobb got a horse from the livery and set off.

He hadn't got very far down the trail when he realized he was being followed.

He was instantly wary. He couldn't think of any reason why someone should be following him over what he was doing; unless Heather had another manfriend no one knew about and who didn't want her brought back to face trial. But there were plenty of people about only too willing to gun down a lawman without needing an excuse.

He pulled off to one side of the trail under the shelter of some stunted pine trees. Sitting still, he pulled out his gun. He didn't have long to wait. The other rider came on, slowly but steadily. As he passed by, Cobb jigged his horse forward. The man, who was young and had a dark, straggly beard, looked like a cowboy. That didn't mean anything.

'Hold it right there!'

The cowboy came to a startled halt and pulled his horse round to face Cobb. As he did so, Cobb saw his hand reaching for the bolstered Colt.

'Wouldn't do that iffen I was you,' Zac said and raised his own gun, thumb reaching to pull back the hammer.

The cowboy went white and immediately flung his arms up in the air. 'Didn't mean no harm, mister,' he stammered.

'Why did you go for your gun?'

'Thought you was about to rob me. Are you? I ain't got much money on me but you're welcome to what I have if you let me go.'

'What's your name?'

'Cal Reeves.'

'Well, Mr Reeves, I might let you go if you tell me why you were following me?'

'Following you?' He sounded puzzled. 'I wasn't. I'm on my way back home from

Glory. Honest, mister. Where I work is just over the hill.'

Cobb uncocked the revolver but carefully kept hold of it. 'All right, get on. But don't let me see you again. Iffen I do, I shoot first then ask the questions, understand?'

'Yeah, mister, sure. Sorry.' Looking all too relieved at being allowed to go, Reeves rode away, slowly at first, and then, after one quick glance back to make sure Cobb had stayed where he was, putting the horse into a trot. He soon disappeared amongst the trees.

Cobb waited where he was for a few minutes more, in case Reeves tried to double back.

He was probably being paranoid. The cowboy looked exactly like what he'd said he was. What Cobb needed was a rest from hunting outlaws. All the same, Bellington's detectives made a lot of enemies in a lot of different places. There was no point in taking chances. He'd watch his back trail the rest of the way to Copper City.

FOUR

Gary Travis pushed open the saloon door. Followed by his younger brother, Neil, he shoved his way through the crowds of men—cowboys, miners, outlaws and the like—and the few girls who entertained them, to the bar. Although only just gone seven, life was already getting into its swing. Batty's saloon, like the rest of Copper City, was rowdy and threatened, nightly, to get out of control.

It was the sort of place where Travis liked to think he was at home.

'Two beers,' he ordered, when he finally caught the bartender's eye. 'And,' he added to Neil, 'drink it slow. We ain't got the money to have more'n one each and still have enough left over to get in a gambling game.'

'OK,' Neil agreed moodily. That was the trouble with being small-time outlaws—there

44

was never enough money to do or have anything.

And small-time thieves was what they were and would probably always be.

Their last robbery was of a store just outside of town. It could hardly be called successful. During it they had almost been knifed by the storeowner's Apache wife and the amount they got was just seven dollars. With this they had headed for Copper City, which Gary had heard was a wide open, rip-roaring town. It probably was—if there was money to spend. As far as the Travis brothers were concerned their seven dollars had vanished on drink, a couple of meals at the café and a girl each last night, while Neil had bought himself a new shirt. That was it. Apart from a few coins, it had all gone.

Tonight, if Gary wasn't lucky at cards, and chances were he wouldn't be, Neil knew they'd be thrown out of the boarding-house where they shared a room, and have to sleep in the stables again; they'd have to go without breakfast. A girl would be out of the question.

And, worse, it would mean that Gary would be thinking about another robbery; the unthinkable alternative being to get a job. Gary would never agree to working for a living, and Neil wasn't any too enthusiastic either.

Gary might win when he played poker but most likely only if he cheated, otherwise he'd probably lose everything.

'What's up with you?' Travis asked nastily, squeezing Neil's arm.

'Nothing.'

'Good. Better not be. I'm doing my best for you, like Pa would have wanted, and I don't want you going against me. Love and gratitude are all I ask for.'

Neil didn't bother to say anything. Gary only got meaner if he was told he was talking hogwash.

The two brothers were alike in neither looks nor temperament.

Gary Travis was thirty, a big, burly man with tangled brown hair and a bushy brown beard. He dressed untidily in whatever he could find. He was also a bully, like his father before him, and liked using his fists and feet, especially on his younger brother, who presented an easy and readily available target.

Neil was just turned twenty-one, and there were often times when he thought he wouldn't make it to twenty-two. His brown hair was long, hanging to below his shoulders and he was trying to grow a moustache in order to make himself appear older but without a great deal of success. Almost as tall as Gary, he was lean and he hoped good-looking enough to appeal to the ladies. He liked to dress as well as he could afford, which wasn't as well as he'd have liked, and his proudest possessions were three highly colourful vests.

Gary liked the life they led. He was quite content to laze away his days doing nothing, interspersed with a robbery now and then to get some necessary money, which he then spent on enjoying himself. But Neil wasn't any too sure that there wasn't something better, although what that was and how to achieve it he didn't know.

When their father died ten years earlier,

Gary had accepted responsibility for his younger brother. Their mother had, understandably, run away many years before. Neil had been scared of his father, a casual labourer who, in his spare time, was a hellfire preacher, fond of beating the devil out of his sons, in case they had any of their wicked mother in them.

He was even more scared of Gary.

But he knew no other way of life, except that provided by his brother. And he felt sure, from having been told so often, that he wasn't clever enough to make his own way in the world. Without Gary there to look after him, jail or the gallows was surely his near future.

Gary Travis turned round, leaning back against the bar, staring round the low-ceilinged room. Tobacco smoke hung like a cloud over everything; there was the strong smell of bad whiskey; the floor hadn't been swept for sometime. Who cared about that? As well as a roulette wheel, several card games were in progress. A couple were clearly being run by professional cardsharps who were fleecing the other players as hard as they could go; another couple involved much too large stakes—it was no good joining in any of them. But...yeah, over in the far corner.

Four men with small piles of coins in front of them, no sign of a cardsharp or even a house gambler. Just someone who looked like a clerk or some such, a couple of cowboys and a miner. Not even a desperado willing to pull his gun for the sake of a few dollars.

'I'm going over there,' he said to Neil, who had followed the direction of his brother's gaze.

'Are you sure you wanna gamble? If you cheat, with this lot here, it'll mean a shooting or a hanging for sure.'

'I don't need to cheat,' Travis lied huffily. ''Sides, kid, you can come over with me and make sure none of the bastards discovers what I'm up to.'

Reluctantly Neil went over with his brother to the gamblers, who agreed to let Gary sit in with them. Even better they made no remark about the couple of cents and few dimes he put on the table. They clearly didn't have much more themselves. The miner dealt the cards and they began to play.

After a while it looked as if it would be all right; that probably Gary wouldn't need to cheat. None of the players was very good, bluffing when they should have called, calling when they should have bluffed. For a change Travis was the best player of the lot and soon his winnings mounted steadily.

'Hey kid,' he called, 'get me a drink.' And he threw some coins at Neil. 'Not a damn beer either. Make it a double whiskey.'

'You sure?'

'Yeah, I'm goddamned well sure! Get it!'

When Neil brought back Gary's drink, he said, 'Perhaps I oughta take your place. You can go somewhere and drink in peace then.'

Travis laughed. 'You! Don't be so goddamn stupid. You're as goddamn useless at gambling as you are at everything goddamn else.' Clearly he wasn't in a good mood, despite his luck at poker, and clearly his mood would get worse if he continued drinking double whiskies. It always did.

Wisely, Neil decided to leave him to it and go and talk to one of the girls. Maybe if Gary's luck held out there would be enough cash for him to go to bed with her. But, as usual, Neil counted his chickens before they could be hatched. About nine o'clock a lot of drink had already been consumed and was making normally aggressive men even worse. It was then that a commotion—yells, a thump or two, a scream—broke out from the corner where Travis was sitting.

'Oh, goddammit!' Neil muttered under his breath. He half thought about leaving Gary to get on with whatever trouble he'd started. But if he did that he'd be in worse trouble with Gary than he would be with anyone in the saloon.

As everyone else gathered round, straining their necks to gawp at what was going on, Neil pushed over towards where his brother was causing havoc.

Face red with anger and drink, Travis

had stood up and had one of the cowboys in a stranglehold against him. They were struggling together but Travis was by far the stronger and already the cowboy's eyes were bulging as he clawed helplessly at the arm round his neck. Travis was shouting something about a cheating sonofabitch, which was good coming from him, but it wouldn't have mattered whether the cowboy had cheated or not, Travis simply wanted a fight.

'Gary!' Neil added his own yell to the other shouts. 'Leave him be.'

He leapt towards his brother, catching at his arm. At the same time, the cowboy's friend in the game, who had so far been watching in wide-eyed horror, also decided to take a hand. The cowboy jumped in and all four went down on the floor, knocking over tables and chairs as they did so.

That was the signal for a general mêlee to start up, the inhabitants of Batty's always being on the look-out for any chance of a good fight.

Someone flung a punch at his neighbour, beer was spilled, the miner began to scrabble around on the floor for any loose coins.

One of the bartenders, a shaven-headed individual, who appreciated a fight as much as the next man, dived forward wielding a club. It caught Neil hard on the arm. Howling in pain, losing all feeling in arm and hand, Neil reeled away from where he'd been trying to pull Travis off his victim.

'That's the bastard!' He heard a shout and more of the cowboy's buddies came pounding down from upstairs where they'd been enjoying the girls' favours, in order to avenge their friend, 'Get him!'

Urged on by others who couldn't have cared less about the identity of the guilty party, they mistook Neil for the assailant and he found himself being borne to the ground by a variety of the saloon's inhabitants. With no love lost between cowboys and miners, everyone tried to punch one another while they all tried to punch Neil.

Crushed beneath their weight, he couldn't do anything, either to hit back at them or even defend himself. His arm hurt from the club's blow, his hat was gone and his long hair was being pulled so hard he felt sure it was going to come out at the roots. The sleeve of his new shirt was torn all down one side.

Then just as everyone was having a real swell time, the boom of one barrel of a shot-gun echoed round the room, sending showers of dirt and plaster down on the heads of the combatants.

'Hold it, right, there!' Marshal Newborn yelled, which was a bit unnecessary because the shot had caused them all to come to an abrupt halt in what they were doing. Drunk, aggressive and excited they all might be but no one was foolish enough to want to go up against a shot-gun.

Together with the bartender, who made a lot of use of his club, Newborn dragged bodies up from the floor, shoving them out of the way. Until at the bottom he came across Neil.

'That's the troublemaker!' the bartender accused, picking on Neil simply because earlier he'd been seen with Travis. Several of the others nodded and shouted agreement.

Newborn caught hold of the collar of Neil's shirt, dragging him to his feet, causing the collar to rip as well as the sleeve. 'OK, so what's all this about?'

'I didn't do anything.' Through bloodied lips, Neil tried to protest his innocence. 'I was trying to stop it.'

'It was him!'

'He started it!'

Desperately Neil looked round for his brother. Naturally now that he was needed the bastard was nowhere to be seen. It was typical of Gary that he was the one who'd caused the fight, then when things turned nasty he'd slipped away, leaving Neil not only to take the blows but also the blame.

'Come along, son,' Newborn said. 'You'd better come and cool your heels in the jail cell for the night.'

Grumpily Neil stooped to pick up his hat. His arm gripped by the marshal he allowed himself to be led through the saloon and out into the cool night air.

Life, he decided, was pretty goddamned unfair.

FIVE

Cobb didn't think much of Copper City. Situated at the head of a short valley, it seemed to consist only of a redlight district. At ten o'clock at night, lights and noise spilled out across the dusty street, numerous horses were tied up at the rails outside the saloons and groups of young men staggered along, arms round one another, looking for fun and trouble. A shot rang out but no one took any notice.

Cobb's horse weaved its way down the centre of the street, which Cobb reckoned was about the safest place to be, away from the shadows of dark alleyways, and then turned into a quiet and very short street. Here the only lights burning were in the porch of a boarding-house and in the marshal's office.

Zac was tired. He'd been riding most

of the day and although no further danger had threatened, he'd been on the alert for most of that time. He wanted nothing more than to go to bed, even if the boarding-house didn't look much better than the rest of the town. Before doing so, he decided he ought to put duty before sleep and let Marshal Newborn know he'd arrived.

Jack Newborn looked to Cobb a bit like the town he protected—fighting a losing battle and rapidly giving in. At around sixty he probably wasn't all that bothered and was just filling in time until he could retire. Still he greeted Cobb enthusiastically enough.

'You got here quick. Did you ride? You ain't gonna ride back with the girl are you?'

'No. I'll take the stage. There is one leaves tomorrow isn't there?' Cobb hoped he didn't sound as anxious as he felt.

'Yeah. Leaves every morning sharp at nine, that is if the driver's sober.'

'Good. I suppose there won't be any trouble getting tickets?'

Newborn laughed. 'No. I know most people want to leave Copper City as soon as they can but then not that many people arrive here in the first place. Don't worry, Mr Cobb, I'm up and about early, I'll go and buy your tickets once the stage office is open.'

'Thanks.'

'You can stable your horse at the livery and I'll make arrangements to get it back to Glory some time. Now, do you wanna see Miss Watkins? She ain't asleep.'

'How's she taking it all?'

'Angry about being turned in for the money. Angry that her lover posted a reward on her and resigned to being taken back. She won't cause you any trouble.'

'I know.'

Newborn looked at Cobb and decided he wouldn't like to be a prisoner of the serious young man.

The cells were situated beyond a door at the rear of the office. There were five of them, two of which were occupied. One by a sulky looking young man, with the beginnings of a black eye and extremely long hair, which made Cobb itch for a pair of scissors; and the other by Miss Heather Watkins.

Cobb hadn't known exactly what to expect but Heather certainly looked much younger, prettier and more innocent than most other prostitutes he'd ever come across. She was twenty-three, short and very slim, although with all the lumps and bumps in the right places, shown off by her tight-fitting skirt and jacket. Her hair was fair and curly, hanging halfway down her back and she had blue eyes. The only thing spoiling her prettiness was that she looked angry, and scared.

'Miss Watkins,' Newborn said and she got to her feet approaching the bars. 'This is Mr Cobb, he works for Bellington's Detective Agency. He's taking you back to Glory.'

Politely Cobb touched his hat. 'Ma'am.'

'I'm innocent of these charges,' Heather immediately said. 'I never shot anyone. You've got to believe me.'

Cobb didn't take any notice. Most criminals he'd ever known always protested their innocence, even those caught with the gun in their hand in the middle of a bank robbery. It was a misunderstanding, they'd been forced into it; they could always come up with fancy excuses to disguise the fact that they were breaking the law.

'You can't take me back.'

'I'm sorry, ma'am. Marshal Hepworth has put out a warrant for your arrest and it's up to me to deliver you to him.'

'Stupid bastard,' Heather muttered.

'Now, now, there's no need for that kinda talk. Mr Cobb is just doing his job,' Newborn said. 'You'd better go to sleep now. Get some rest. You'll be leaving early in the morning.'

When the two lawmen had gone out, Neil said, 'What do they want you for?' He liked young women, especially pretty ones, and he didn't think she could have done anything much wrong.

'Murder.'

'Oh,' he said, his illusions shattered.

'But like I told that stupid detective I didn't do it.'

60

Neil took as little notice as Cobb of that.

'I wouldn't even be here if my so-called friend hadn't betrayed me.'

'And I wouldn't be here if it wasn't for my goddamned brother.'

'What are you here for then?'

'Fighting in the saloon. I expect to be out come morning. To keep me here or charge me with anything will cause that marshal too much effort. He just wanted to get me out of the way and let things get back to normal.'

'You look as if you got the worst of it anyway.'

'I did.'

'The law is exceedingly stupid.' And with this statement, with which Neil could only agree, Heather went over to the bunk, lay down, pulled the blanket over her head and tried to go to sleep.

'Is the telegraph office open?' Cobb asked Newborn.

'Not at this time of night. Won't be open until tomorrow morning. Want me to send a telegraph for you?'

'If you don't mind. I want to confirm with Marshal Hepworth that the prisoner is Heather Watkins and that I'll be returning on the stage. By the way is the boarding-house the only place to stay?'

'It is lessen you want to sleep in one of the saloons or at the livery. Take a chance on the boarding-house iffen I was you.'

'Thanks. 'Night, see you in the morning.'

With a certain sense of foreboding about what he'd find at the boarding-house, Cobb wondered whether to go along to one of the saloons and have a couple of drinks to help him sleep. He decided against it. Mr Bellington didn't mind his detectives having the odd drink, although he didn't approve of drunks, but he didn't particularly like them drinking in places as notorious as this redlight district obviously was, where they might be corrupted, or shot, by the people they met. Besides he had a feeling he'd need to be sober and alert to handle Miss Watkins.

'Do you want me to go to the Circle B

and tell Mr Bartlett about Heather being found?' Tommy Reynolds asked when the Copper City telegraph was delivered to Hepworth.

'No, I'll go myself.'

'You sure you're OK?'

'Yeah. I'm feeling a lot better today but I'll take the buckboard, that'll be easier than riding.' Hepworth wasn't all that sure he could make it all the way out to the ranch and back, at least not without suffering a certain amount of pain. But he wanted to go himself so he could impress upon Bartlett that this was a matter for the law.

Zac Cobb went down to the jail house, sober but not exactly alert. He'd been right about that damn boarding-house. He'd hardly slept all night. The bed had been hard and uncomfortable and full of things that kept him awake, making him itch. Through the paper-thin partitions of the rooms on either side of his had come the sound of hefty snoring. While in the street the inhabitants of the redlight district had

63

celebrated way into the early hours, all of them seeming to pass the boarding-house on their way home.

And this morning's breakfast, provided by the landlady, had consisted of greasy bacon, a greasy egg and black coffee so strong Cobb was tempted to stand his spoon up in it.

Thus he wasn't in the best of moods.

In the marshal's office a burly looking man was waiting by the desk as Newborn led out the young man who'd occupied a cell the night before.

'My advice to you two is to leave town,' Newborn said, handing over the young man's gunbelt. 'I don't want any more trouble and iffen you hang around I'll be keeping an eye on you both and I might just not like what I see.'

'Don't worry, we're going,' Gary Travis said. 'Come on, Neil, let's get outa this damn unfriendly town.'

'Who were they?' Cobb asked as the door closed behind them. 'Oh a pair of no-hopers called Travis. They ain't particularly bright. I've gotta feeling that if I looked hard enough I might even find a warrant out on 'em.'

'They're thieves, then?'

'Probably, but if so they ain't very good at it. For the few days they've been here they ain't hardly had any money. Now I reckon it's run out so they'll head elsewhere, robbing a couple of lonely travellers as they go.' Newborn shrugged. 'Pair of idiots. They ain't worth worrying about. I expect they'll be killed in an attempted robbery before long and so save the taxpayers the cost of keeping 'em in jail.' Cobb wasn't sure that Mr Bellington would approve of such a lax attitude towards the law, even if Newborn was right about the ineptness of the lawbreakers. However, he decided that right now it wasn't any of his business either and promptly forgot all about the Travis brothers as well.

'Where we going?' Neil asked as he followed Gary down the street.

'Well, thanks to you, we've gotta get out of town!'

'What do you mean, thanks to me?'

'You're the one got in trouble with the law and ended up in a cell. Now that sonofabitch marshal knows us. Any trouble he'll be blaming us. What's more in all that fighting last night I managed to lose the money I'd won.'

'That wasn't my fault. I wasn't the one started the fight.'

'You were the one interfered,' Travis glared. 'Serve you right if I left you here alone and went on my own goddamn way.'

'Serve you right if I stopped here and let you go,' Neil retorted.

'Don't get smart with me,' Travis snarled and hit Neil round the side of his head with a loud crack.

Neil fell forward on to his knees and just managed to squirm out of the way of Travis's boot as his foot attempted to make contact with Neil's ribs. Clearly a night of sleeping it off hadn't improved his disposition and wisely Neil decided to keep quiet.

Satisfied that he'd cowed his brother,

Travis's spurt of temper died as quickly as it had arisen. And, helping Neil to his feet, he dusted him down, patted his arm, and went over to the livery stable owner to see about their horses.

Neil watched him go, wondering if he'd ever be free of his brother and his unpredictable temper. He doubted it. In his heart he knew he'd never get up the courage to leave him and go his own way.

'So where are we off to?' Neil asked again as he swung up on the horse's back.

'Glory. I've heard that's a real fine town.'

'We ain't gonna rob anyone there are we?' Neil asked in a bit of a panic. He was always scared that Gary would get ideas above their station and want to rob a bank or something.

'Course we ain't! Don't be so damn stupid! Too much law in Glory, good law too. Don't worry, Neil, I've got a plan.'

That really did cause Neil's heart to sink. Gary's plans seldom turned out the way they were meant and he didn't like the way his brother was smiling. It was quite likely that one day in the near future he would be free of Gary—by getting shot!

SIX

'Handcuffs!' Heather exclaimed. 'You can't make me wear handcuffs! Everyone will think I've done something wrong!'

Cobb ignored her. He put one cuff round her right wrist and secured the other round his left wrist, leaving his gunhand free, and put the key in his vest pocket. Then, shaking hands with Marshal Newborn, he flung his saddle-bags over his shoulder and handed Heather her small reticule. 'Is that all you've got with you?'

'Yes.'

'What about the things you took from your house?'

'I didn't take anything from my house.'

Cobb shrugged. Her baggage, or rather

68

lack of it, was no concern of his.

'There's no need for this,' Heather said as they started down the road, the morning already warm and sunny. 'I haven't done anything.'

'Look, Miss Watkins, frankly I believe you shot Mr Tomlin but maybe if you flash your pretty eyes at judge and jury you'll be able to convince them that you're innocent or at least had a good reason for doing it. It's nothing to do with me. I'm just taking you to Glory and so long as all goes to plan, we should be there by late this evening. We're just going to have to get along till then. But I have certain rules and as I'm the lawman and you're my prisoner you're going to have to follow them.'

Heather sighed heavily. 'What are they?'

'Just that you behave yourself, keep quiet and act polite and don't do anything silly. That way you won't get hurt.'

'And if I try anything silly?'

'Then the fact that you're a woman won't make no never mind to me.'

'Did anyone ever tell you you were a bully?'

'I'm practical. You've already shot one man. I'm not about to take the chance that you might shoot another, which is me. Understand?'

'Yes. If I promise I won't try to escape will you take these handcuffs off?' But one look at Cobb's face told her that all her pleas would be a waste of time. She was going to have to suffer the indignity of making the journey chained to him.

Luckily for Heather there weren't many people around to see her and Cobb walking down the street, but two other passengers were waiting for the stage. One was a matronly, schoolma'am type, dressed all in black from bonnet to boots. When Cobb and Heather came round the corner into the yard a look of disgust came on to her face and quickly she drew her skirts tighter about her, putting her feet together, as if fearing contamination.

The other was a man in his last forties. He had a large paunch with a gold watchchain lying across it. Cobb put him down as a rich and pompous rancher. From the glance he gave Heather, which was both appreciative and cunning, once he had recognized her for what she was, Cobb felt he could have trouble with him.

Presumably they had been staying at the boarding-house but wisely hadn't bothered about breakfast.

'Hello there, Deputy,' the man said, all smiles and being taken in by the badge Cobb wore. 'What have we got here then? Someone been a naughty girl has she?'

Both Heather and the woman scowled, but for obviously different reasons.

'Are you going to Glory?'

Cobb didn't really want to reply but saw no alternative. Mr Bellington liked his deputies to be polite to the law-abiding citizenry. 'Yes.'

'Then we shall all be together for all of the way.'

'Unfortunately,' said the woman.

'By the way, I'm Henry Potter,' the rancher introduced himself. 'And this is...I'm sorry I don't know your name,' he added to the schoolma'am, clearly not having been interested in making her acquaintance.

'It's Miss Haynes.'

Cobb was forced to introduce himself and Heather.

'What's she wanted for, Mr Cobb?' Potter winked. 'The usual, I expect?'

'Sort of.'

'I think it's disgusting that we should be expected to travel with such a disgrace to womanhood! When I purchased my ticket this morning I certainly wasn't informed that one of my companions was going to be a...' Miss Haynes couldn't finish but sank back on the bench as if she was about to swoon.

Heather had so far been quiet during this exchange, now she said,'Don't worry, Miss Haynes, I don't want to travel with you either. Dried up old prune!'

'Well really!' Miss Haynes exclaimed.

'Be quiet!' Cobb warned Heather and wondered if it might not be better to hire a couple of horses after all.

'She started it!' Heather said furiously.

72

'I don't care who started it. I said be quiet.'

Luckily in the middle of this argument, the stagecoach arrived. It clattered into the yard, pulled by four horses, the wheels turning, catching the morning sun. There was the jingle of harness and a rising dust that threatened to cover everything. With a yell at the animals and the squeal of the brake, the driver brought the coach to a halt, inches from where the passengers waited.

'Howdy there, folks!' The driver jumped down, while the guard remained on his perch eyeing them all with lofty disdain. Although early in the day, the driver, an elderly man with long grey whiskers, already had the smell of whiskey on his breath. 'Just the four of you today?' he added. 'Here ma'am let me help you with that.' And he picked up Miss Haynes's bag stowing it in the boot.

'Hey you!' the guard called down. 'You with the badge.'

'Yes?'

He nodded at Heather. 'She ain't going

to cause any trouble is she?'

'No.'

'No, I'm not,' Heather said, getting highly fed up with everyone talking about her as if she wasn't there. 'This is all a mistake. I haven't done anything.'

Cobb handed over his saddle-bags to the driver and then pushed Heather up into the coach. 'Sit by the window.'

Heather was glad to do so, for it meant she was well away from Potter's leering eyes and Miss Haynes's glare as they sat opposite.

'I'm Jed Sykes.' The driver poked his head in the coach door. 'Guard's Pete Groves. Got three stops to Glory. With a good road, good weather and good luck we should be there by about seven this evening.'

'What did he mean good luck?' Miss Haynes asked nervously.

'Outlaws could attack us,' Potter said. At the woman's little cry of fright, he patted her hand. 'Don't fret, dear lady. You'll be quite safe. I'm told no robbers have attacked this line in years but if they should be foolish enough to do so then you have not only the guard but Mr Cobb and myself to protect you.'

'Oh God,' Heather spoke under her breath.

With a yell and a curse that brought a blush to Miss Haynes's cheeks, the driver whipped up his team. The horses started forward, the coach swung round in a half circle and they were out of the yard and driving through the as yet almost deserted streets of Copper City. Once beyond the town limits the coach quickly picked up speed and was soon bowling along, fast although not all that comfortably, the passengers jouncing round in their seats. Beyond the windows stretched the vast reaches of empty desert, the only splashes of colour the endless sagebrush and clumps of mesquite plant.

Potter was clearly the type who couldn't keep quiet for very long. After a short while, he turned to Miss Haynes and in a hearty voice, said, 'Well, dear lady, what are you doing out here in Arizona? It doesn't really seem as if you're at home here. You appear, if you don't mind me saying so, rather nervous.' He laughed.

Miss Haynes blushed. 'I will admit, Mr Potter, that I'm not used to the West at all. I have lived most of my life in San Francisco, such a beautiful town. I was a governess there to some delightful children...'

'Poor kids,' Heather muttered and Cobb kicked her hard.

'...but now they are grown up and no longer need me. My employer was kind enough to suggest similar employment with his brother's family in Phoenix. And that is where I am going. However, I'm not sure how I'm going to like it. I hope it's nothing like Copper City. One night there while I waited for this change of stagecoach was quite bad enough. Such a rough place and such rough people. I couldn't bear it if Phoenix was the same.'

'It isn't,' said Cobb. 'But it is very hot.'

'And there are wild Indians and outlaws,' Heather added wickedly.

'Don't take any notice,' Cobb said

crossly, wondering why on earth Marshal Hepworth had considered Heather a nice young lady when she was proving to be such a pain in the ass. 'The Indians and outlaws aren't likely to attack a town the size of Phoenix. You'll be all right. And you, Potter, are you on your way home?' He wasn't really all that interested but talking to the other passengers passed the time on a wearying journey.

'That's right. My ranch is near Tucson. So my dear Miss Haynes we shall probably be going on together from Glory.'

'I hope so,' Miss Haynes fluttered her eyelashes nervously. 'This is such a long journey, so confusing. It would be nice to have a companion.'

'I've been buying beef up in Montana. My ramrod and the crew are bringing them back while I go on ahead and make arrangements for their arrival.'

'So exciting! Such colourful terms! Perhaps it won't be so bad after all. And, Mr Cobb, are you really a deputy?'

'No. I'm a private detective but I'm

working for the marshal in Glory at the moment.' Cobb, ever ready to boast, told them all a little about Bellington's Detective Agency and his part in it.

'What made you become a detective?' Heather asked.

'I'm not sure, not really.' His background was the one thing Cobb didn't like to talk about.

His mother's family were originally farmers from Ohio. When he was three his father, a spendthrift and a drifter who had married Zac's mother against her parents' wishes, decided he'd had enough of being poor and, although his mother hadn't wanted to, they'd moved west. Things still hadn't worked out and several more moves followed. His father had soon turned to drink and had been killed in a bar brawl. His mother went back to Ohio and her family. Zac was eighteen by then, and, liking the West, its freedom and the wide-open skies, had stayed on.

In just one respect he was like his father—he didn't like farming. So he decided on a whim, simply because the town he was in wanted a deputy marshal, to try his hand at being a lawman. Somewhat to his surprise he'd taken to it straightaway and been good at it too. He'd been working as a deputy sheriff in Cheyenne when he was recruited by the local Bellington's agent.

But he didn't like telling anyone that his father had been a drunk and his mother meek and downtrodden, and he had a shortened version of the truth he used on occasions such as this.

With all the talk it seemed only a short while later that they pulled into the relay station.

'Time here to stretch your legs,' Sykes said, opening the door and helping them out. 'Use the privy out back if you like. It's all right ma'am,' he added to Miss Haynes, 'around noon we make a longer stop. There'll be time then for something to eat and to freshen up.'

When Potter and Miss Haynes went round to use the privy, Heather complained

79

to Cobb 'That awful man hasn't stopped leering at me.'

'You should be used to that in your line of work.'

'Well I'm not! Don't be so nasty. You won't let him touch me, will you?'

'Of course I won't!'

'Mr Cobb, please won't you reconsider all this? It is a mistake truly. I didn't kill anyone. You could let me go. I could wait here and catch the stage going back the other way. This is my last chance. No one need know. I don't want to go back to Glory.'

'Sorry.'

'I wouldn't mind if you did more than leer at me.' Heather pressed close to him, stroking his arm with her hand.

'Miss Watkins, I'm a Bellington's detective!' Cobb sounded quite shocked.

'Don't you want me?'

'Not particularly. And we can't be bribed, not by any sort of offer.'

'Oh!' Heather made a disgusted, disappointed sound in her throat, but whether it was disappointment because Cobb didn't want her or because he wouldn't let her go he didn't know, although he suspected the latter.

'Ready to go!' Sykes called out.

The passengers hurried back to the stage, Cobb pulling Heather after him. By now the conversation seemed to be at an end, even Potter was quiet and Heather sat with a sullen look on her face. So Zac decided to catch up on his sleep. Pulling his hat down over his face, he closed his eyes.

'How can you?' Miss Haynes cried. 'You're responsible for a prisoner. She might do something terrible if you don't watch her.'

'No she won't.' Cobb momentarily held up his hand that was cuffed to Heather. Then lulled by the rocking of the stage he fell asleep.

Not that he got much rest.

About a mile down the road, just where Sykes slowed the horses to take the bend round a low butte, several shots rang out. And a voice demanded that they come to a halt.

SEVEN

'Well, hi there, Marshal!' Bartlett greeted Hepworth as he drew the buckboard to a halt in front of the ranchhouse. 'Good to see you out and about again. You all right now?'

'More or less.' However, it was with considerable effort that Hepworth didn't groan as he eased himself down from the buckboard seat. He couldn't prevent himself wincing but if Bartlett noticed he pretended he didn't.

Bartlett led the way towards the house. 'I saw you at Norman's funeral but I didn't speak to you because you looked pretty busy handling the crowd that came out for him.' He shook his head. 'It was a sad and unnecessary occasion but at least you made sure it went off in a dignified manner. Now,' he added, pouring out whiskey for them both, 'I hope you've got some good news.'

'Heather Watkins has been found. She was hiding in Copper City. Mr Cobb, you know the Bellington's detective, is bringing her back. They're coming by stage. They should arrive some time this evening.'

'That certainly is good news! Well done!'

'Look, Robin, I know how you feel an' all but I don't want you taking the law into your own hands over this. Mr Cobb is quite capable of bringing her back and I'm quite capable of handling her once she's in the Glory jail. And I'll be the one to ask the questions as to why she did it. Understand?'

'Don't worry, Marshal. I admit I'm angry and bewildered over this. Not only because I thought Heather was faithful to me, I certainly paid the little bitch enough, but also because she shot poor Norman...'

'She may have had reason,' Hepworth pointed out.

'Yeah or it may have been greed on her part! However, whatever the truth of the matter is, I'm certainly not going to form a lynching party or try to punish Heather in any way. It'll be a matter for the law.'

'That's all I wanted to hear.' Hepworth spoke more sincerely than he felt and decided to take Bartlett's words with a pinch of salt and keep an eye on him and his men.

'I'm real busy out here at the moment.' Bartlett refilled their glasses. 'But I'll come into Glory as soon as I can, both to see Heather for myself and also to pay the reward I promised. I still don't understand why it happened but I feel better now Heather has been caught. At least I can believe Norman is resting easy.'

There being no more to be said and feeling that such pious sentiments didn't sit all that well on someone like Bartlett who never went to church, Hepworth climbed back on to the buckboard for the long journey back to town.

As he disappeared over the horizon, Dean Morrow strode up from the direction of the bunkhouse. 'What was all that about, Robin?'

'Come on inside and I'll tell you.'

The shots, as well as the screams of both Heather and Miss Haynes, jerked Cobb awake from his slumbers. Before he could do anything there was another shot and a yell of 'Don't be stupid!' and the coach came to such an abrupt halt that the passengers had difficulty in keeping their seats.

Then, even as Cobb was dragging his gun out of its holster, the door was flung open and one of the robbers stuck a revolver inside, and shouted, 'Don't try anything foolish, folks.'

Despite Potter's earlier reassurance to the nervous Miss Haynes, the fact that there were four armed men present wasn't going to prevent the stage from being robbed. Indeed Potter was the first to fling his arms in the air as he cowered behind the ashen-faced governess. And faced by an already drawn gun, practically stuck up his nose, Cobb couldn't do anything but what he was told either.

'Let's get outa the stage,' the man said.

He wore a bandanna covering the lower half of his face, only his excited eyes visible between that and his hat, which was pulled down over his forehead.

Even so Cobb felt sure there was something familiar about him and when he got out of the coach and saw the second robber, still on his horse, keeping a gun pointed at guard and driver, he was certain. Neither hat nor bandanna could hide the long straight hair or the blackened eye.

It was the Travis brothers!

'Please don't hurt us,' Miss Haynes begged.

'No one'll get hurt so long as they do what they're told. What the hell's this?' Travis had seen Cobb and Heather handcuffed together. 'You a goddamn lawman?'

'Sure he is,' Neil said from his horse. 'He was in Copper City yesterday. You fool, Gary, we're robbing a stage with a lawman on board!' There was a rising note of panic in his voice.

'Shut your damn mouth, kid. It don't

make no never mind, we've still got the drop on him,' Travis giggled. He poked Cobb in the chest with his gun. Ain't we lawman?'

'For now.' There was an edge to Cobb's voice that a wiser man than Travis might have taken note of and done what he could to avoid.

'Take your gun out and drop it on the ground,' Travis ordered, too busy enjoying the power he held to notice any threat to his future wellbeing. 'You too Mr Rancher. Slowly now!'

'I don't know why you're robbing us,' Pete Groves said. 'We ain't carrying anything 'cept passengers. You're wasting your time.'

'I don't know about that,' Cobb taunted. 'These two haven't got a couple of dimes between them so however little we give them is going to seem like a fortune.'

'Shut up. Just start handing over your money. All of it.' Travis started with Heather. 'Come on, missy, you musta earned a lot in your time.'

'Maybe but I haven't got any of it with

me.' Heather opened the purse she carried. It was empty.

Travis scowled, moving on to Cobb, poking him in the chest again. 'What you got then, lawman?'

Most of Cobb's money was back in Glory in the marshal's safe. He'd only brought enough for expenses. And that had been eaten into by the boarding-house and the purchase of two stage tickets. Thus the money he handed over to Travis didn't amount to much.

'Please don't hurt me, please. Here take my money,' Miss Haynes cried when Travis pointed the gun at her. She pushed her purse in his outstretched hand. 'Take it all. And leave us alone. Let us go. You won't kill us, will you?'

'Of course they won't,' Cobb said. 'They're not killers, just fools.'

Travis took no notice because Potter, trembling with fear, gave him a wallet stuffed with dollar bills. He peered into it, lips moving as he tried to count what was there. With a cry of triumph he looked towards Neil. 'We're rich! There must be over fifty dollars in here!'

'Just take it and go,' Potter urged.

'And your watch, fat man.'

'Oh no...'

'Come on hand it over!' Travis cocked the revolver causing Miss Haynes to fall back against Cobb in a half faint.

'For Chrissakes, Gary, forget it,' Neil urged. 'We've got enough. Let's just go.'

Good advice, but Travis didn't take it. Instead he reached out and grabbed at the watch chain, pulling it away from Potter's fat stomach. He grinned. 'Thanks for your contribution to our wellbeing, folks. Weren't so painful after all were it?' He poked Cobb once more in the chest with his gun before he holstered it. 'P'raps you'll remember the day you were robbed by Gary Travis!' Putting the watch in the pocket where he'd stuffed the money and Potter's wallet, he sauntered over to his horse.

As soon as he'd mounted, both robbers dug heels into the animals' sides and were away with a pounding of hooves. Within moments they'd disappeared amongst the rocks at the side of the road.

'They've got my money and my watch!' Potter screamed. 'They robbed us! You're meant to be a lawman. You're not letting them get away with it are you?'

'No.' Cobb reached into his pocket for the handcuffs key, quickly freeing his wrist. Snatching up his gun he ran for the rocks, climbing amongst them, hands and feet scrabbling for holds. He was followed by Groves.

When they got to the top the Travis brothers were already galloping across the valley floor. Gary Travis was slightly in front.

'Give me your rifle!' Cobb ordered. Grabbing it from Groves, he stood against a boulder laying the weapon along the top. Aiming carefully he fired.

The crack of the rifle, the smoke of the shot was followed a few moments later by Neil's horse rearing wildly. Neil tumbled backwards out of the saddle and landed with a thump that raised up a cloud of dust. He lay still while the horse, unhurt but frightened, took off at a gallop. Gary

Travis pulled his own animal to a halt, glanced back at his brother, and fled, yet again leaving Neil to whatever fate awaited him.

Cobb sent several shots after him but he was too far away for them to do any good. 'Come on.'

When he and Groves got up to him, Neil was just struggling to sit up. He looked pale and terrified but otherwise unhurt. He'd lost his hat and his long hair had fallen forward over his face.

Holding the rifle steady, Cobb reached out for Neil's gun and handed it to Groves.

'You silly little bastard!' Groves yelled and pointed the gun at Neil's head, finger twitching at the trigger. 'I oughta kill you for what you did!'

'No! Please, mister don't!'

'No!' Cobb said at the same time, knocking the gun down. 'Just because he made a fool of you is no reason to shoot him.'

'The bastard,' Groves repeated and kicked Neil hard in the ribs several times.

Neil groaned as he rolled on to his side trying to curl up in a protective ball.

Cobb let Groves have his fun for a while then said, 'Leave it.'

'What gives you the right to take charge?' Groves asked nastily and went to kick Neil again. 'It's my stagecoach he robbed.'

'And he broke the law and I'm the lawman.' Cobb shoved Groves aside and grabbed for Neil's arm, dragging him to his feet. He flung Neil's hat at him, giving him a push that almost sent him sprawling again. 'You're under arrest, son.' Then he caught his arm in a vice-like grip and with Groves on his other side, Neil, his mind numb with fear, was pushed and pulled back to the stage where the others waited.

'We heard a shot,' Sykes called. 'What happened?'

'We got one of the bastards,' Groves said triumphantly. 'He ain't hurt, more's the pity.'

'Where's my money? Where's my watch?'

Potter yelled and dashed towards Neil. Before anyone could do anything, he lashed out, catching the young man round the side of the face so that Neil stumbled backwards.

Miss Haynes cried out at such violence, hiding her eyes behind her hands.

As Potter looked set to hit Neil again, and thinking that given any encouragement the guard and probably the driver would join in, Cobb caught hold of Potter, pulling him off balance and away. Neil Travis had broken the law and behaved foolishly but Groves had already beaten him up for it, he didn't deserve any more.

'He doesn't have the money or your goddamned watch. You know that. You saw the other one take it. Now leave him alone, this isn't doing any of us any good.' Cobb could feel Neil trembling as he caught his arm again and walked him over to the stage. 'Miss Watkins come here.' He caught hold of the handcuff dangling from Heather's wrist.

'What are you doing?' she cried out.

'You're not chaining me to him are you? Oh you can't!'

But Cobb could.

'He's a common thief,' Heather objected.

'Better than being an uncommon murderer,' Neil said.

'Shut up.' Cobb hit him round the back of his head. 'You'd better be careful. You've seen what the others would like to do to you. I'm all that stands between you and them. Upset me and I might just hand you over to them. I haven't got much time for thieves who rob me.'

Neil glanced at Cobb to see if he meant what he said and then looked down because it seemed he did. 'All right,' he mumbled.

'Is your brother likely to attempt a rescue?'

'I doubt it.' Neil was rather hopeful that Gary wouldn't. He didn't add that to the lawman, feeling sure that he wouldn't understand or believe him.

Cobb doubted it too. Travis hadn't even bothered to stay and find out if his brother was hurt. He'd hardly be likely to try and stop a coach with four men on board, all of whom were now fully alert.

'Come on, folks, let's be on our way,' Sykes said. 'Excitement's over and we've still got a schedule to keep. Come along, Miss Haynes, everything is all right now. You heard what the kid said. We won't see the other one again.'

'And if we do we'll be ready for him this time,' Groves promised. 'He tries anything the kid there is the one I shoot. Hear that boy?'

'Yes, sir.'

Neil sat by Heather, crammed between her and the lawman. He was very scared, and trying not to cry. He was in trouble sure. A stagecoach robbery, even if it was the first one he'd ever committed, was a serious offence. He'd be put in jail. Gary had been in jail a couple of times and was full of tales about the dreadful things that went on there. He'd used that as a way of keeping Neil by his side saying that without him that's where Neil would land up.

Now it looked like it was going to

happen anyway. And it was all Gary's damn fault. Not only because he had run out on him but because it had been his idea in the first place. Neil had wanted no part of it.

'It'll be easy,' Gary promised that morning as they rode away from Copper City.

Easy? Easy!

All right so the guard had been taken by surprise and hadn't put up any resistance but then that lawman had got out of the coach, looking not in the least bit pleased about what was going on. Neil's heart had sunk. All he'd wanted to do was ride away. If Gary had had any sense that's what he would have done.

And now Gary had got away again and here he was, handcuffed to the lawman's other prisoner and on his way to Glory and a jail sentence. That was if he ever got there and that pompous passenger and the guard didn't kill him first. Neil made up his mind not to do anything, not one thing, to annoy or upset Mr Cobb.

EIGHT

'What I want to know is what you're going to do about this,' Potter declared. 'Both I and poor Miss Haynes here have been threatened and robbed. We want some sort of compensation.'

Miss Haynes nodded. 'My poor heart is still thudding and I feel quite sick.'

'It's nothing to do with me,' Cobb protested.

'You've taken responsibility for it.'

'I've taken responsibility for the robber not the robbery. You'll have to take that up with the stagecoach company.'

'It's disgusting,' Miss Haynes used her favourite expression. 'Someone should put a stop to it.'

'Well at least his activities will be put a stop to,' Potter glared at Neil. 'Ought to be strung up.'

'Perhaps, Mr Potter, that's going a bit

too far but I do hope he's put in jail for a very long time. It's disgusting that we are forced to ride in the coach with him. That other depraved creature was bad enough. He's worse. He should be made to ride elsewhere.'

Cobb wondered if it was against Mr Bellington's strict rules to tell two fare-paying, law-abiding stagecoach passengers to shut up or he'd shut them up. Deciding that it probably was he looked resolutely out of the window, trying not to listen as Potter and Miss Haynes thought up ways of ridding the country of its worst elements.

At just gone noon, they rolled into the home station where the horses would again be changed and the passengers allowed to eat and rest for an hour. The station was just a small dot of civilization in the valley floor, surrounded on all sides by the bare, brown scrub of desert, but at least the foothills around Glory, towards which they were headed, had now appeared on the horizon, giving Cobb the hope that the journey would soon be over.

The horses being of much more import-ance than the passengers, the corral, barn and stables were more prominent than the house. This was a one-storey abode building with a small door, tiny windows and a veranda all the way round for shade.

As the coach came to a halt, a young man hurried from the direction of the stables, beginning to undo the harness, while a man and woman, both stringy and middle aged, appeared from the house.

Glad to stretch their legs after the hot, bumpy ride, the passengers got down.

Immediately Groves was there, jabbing at Neil with his rifle. 'You best be good, boy. Bill has a cemetery out back full of the graves of would be trouble-makers.'

'Fat chance I'll have of causing trouble when there are four of you ready to shoot me down,' Neil muttered, but under his breath so that luckily for him no one heard.

'Welcome,' Bill called out. 'Come in, there's plenty of food.'

'And fresh soap and towels for you

ladies,' his wife began and then stopped as she saw that while one of the female passengers might be a lady, the other one was in handcuffs; and, even worse, chained to her was someone under Groves' careful guard.

'What's this?' Bill said, stepping forward. 'We weren't told about this.'

Groves said, 'We didn't know, Bill. Not about the girl, and especially not about this one.' Again he jabbed Neil with the barrel of his gun. 'He tried robbing us.'

'Oh!' the woman cried. 'No one was hurt was they?'

'No, don't worry, Dolly. But the bastard with him got away with the passengers' money.'

'We were robbed and frightened,' Potter blustered. 'I want to know what you're going to do about it.'

'It ain't nothing to do with these folks, sir,' Sykes said. 'You can take it up with the company when we get to Glory.'

'Well, you'd better come in out of the sun,' Dolly said, adding rather dubiously: 'Those two as well I suppose.'

'Who's in charge of 'em?' Bill asked.

'Me.'

'Just keep 'em out of the way. We don't approve of thieves or prostitutes.'

Dolly put her arm round Miss Haynes. 'Come along in, dear, and make yourself comfortable. You must have had a dreadful time.'

'Disgusting! It was bad enough travelling with that woman and then we were robbed...' Miss Haynes's voice trailed away as she followed the station-owner's wife into the house.

'I don't think they like us much.' Heather sounded a bit despondent.

'I don't like you much either,' said Cobb. 'You're both causing me a whole load of trouble I could well do without. I should have been back home in St Louis by now not out in the middle of the damn desert, with a murderess and an idiot for company.'

Bill came up to Cobb and Groves. 'What happened?'

'This one and his brother surprised us back by Black Butte. Got the drop on me

101

before I could do anything. Mr Cobb here says he saw them both in Copper City.'

'A lot of badness comes out of that town.'

'Pair of idiot brothers called Travis.'

'And you say the other got away?'

'Yeah, but there ain't nothing to fear from him. He's long gone.'

'I hope so. At least this one won't be able to steal from innocent folks for a while. All the same, this is a bad business, Pete. The company ain't gonna like it. Do you know how much was stolen?'

'No. But most of whatever it was belonged to Mr Potter.'

'It would have done.' Bill was well able to tell the awkward passengers. 'Well you'd better come in. Have some stew.'

Inside, the house wasn't all that clean but it was at least cool. In the middle of the main room was a long, scratched table with benches on either side. Several places were laid, three of which Dolly had quickly moved right to the far end, away from the others.

'Go on,' Cobb said, shoving Neil hard.

He sat down, facing the pair of them.

'Are we gonna get anything to eat do you think?' Neil asked, taking off his hat and staring anxiously at Bill who had carried in a panful of steaming stew.

'Miss Watkins will because her ticket's been paid for. I'm not sure what the rules are about feeding someone who's robbed the stage.'

'Anyway how can we eat like this?' Heather demanded indicating her and Neil's handcuffed wrists.

'You'll just have to find a way.'

While they were left until last, Bill and Dolly eventually served both the prisoners with coffee and the greasy stew.

'Thank you ma'am,' Neil said politely, but all he got was a tut in return.

The meat was tough, the vegetables almost non-existent but Neil gulped it down and was in time for seconds, the only one brave enough to have another helping. His fear over what was going to happen to him not affecting his appetite.

'You must have been hungry,' Cobb said.

'I ain't had nothing since last night.' And that hadn't exactly been much. Just a piece of bacon and some beans from Copper City's one café.

'Disgusting,' was Miss Haynes's comment on his eating manners.

Cobb waited until everyone else had gone outside then said, 'Come on you two, let's go. I'll have to uncuff you so don't try anything.'

'What would be the point?' Heather asked tartly. 'As you said we're out in the middle of the desert.'

Outside, Dolly had put two bowls of hot water on a bench under the veranda, one for the men, one for the women. Beside each were soap and towels.

Cobb pulled Neil and Heather a little way away while Potter and Miss Haynes did their best to freshen up.

'I'll help you keep an eye on 'em,' Groves said, and stood brandishing the rifle while Cobb washed face and hands.

'You'd both better use the privy,' Cobb said when he'd finished. 'It's a long way to the next stop. Neil, you come with

104

me; Miss Watkins you can have use of the water.'

'Don't I get to wash?' Neil asked.

'One bowl of water and a small piece of soap won't exactly do you much good!'

Cobb undid their handcuffs and, followed by the careful Groves, who wasn't going to make any more mistakes, accompanied Neil round to the back of the house.

Miss Haynes came out of the privy, went red as she saw them and, with a little squeal, ran back to the house.

'You first, I'll be waiting for you. And, Groves, I don't want you shooting him and telling me he was trying to escape. Even you wouldn't be that stupid, would you kid?'

Neil shook his head.

'It's all right, Mr Cobb, I ain't going to shoot him. I'm over that foolishness now. I want to see the little bastard stand trial.'

'He'll do that all right.'

Neil sighed heavily. All right so he'd helped to rob the stage but somehow it didn't seem right that everyone was treating him as if he was both vicious and stupid.

Meanwhile, Heather had washed her hands and splashed the water on her face. Being a fastidious sort of young woman, she would have liked to take off her clothes and wash herself free of all the dust and dirt. She held up the towel in disgust and said to no one in particular but just getting rid of some of her frustration and fright, 'She called this fresh! It's plain dirty! How can I possibly use it?'

'I can see that a young lady like you is used to finer things.' Potter had come up close behind her, making her jump as she felt him breathing down her neck.

Heather glanced up. Cobb and Groves were out by the privy, waiting for Neil. Miss Haynes was talking to the station couple. Sykes was with the boy seeing to the horses. She and Potter were alone. She wasn't scared. She knew how to handle him and besides if he did try anything, a scream from her would bring everyone running.

'I could help you, you know,' Potter went on, stepping even closer. 'That is if you were nice to me.'

'Really, how?' Heather asked. She would not mind using him as he wanted to use her, if it meant escape...but it never would. Copper City was in one direction, Glory in the other. There was nowhere else to go, nowhere for her to escape to; even if there was a horse, water and provisions to escape with. And as for Potter, he would never dare go up against Zac Cobb.

'You be nice to me first and I'll find a way to get you free and away before we reach Glory.'

Potter had no intention of helping her. All he wanted was to make love to her and then forget her.

'Come on, missy, we can go round the back. There's time and they'll wait for us. Miss Haynes might be disgusted but everyone else will understand.'

'Sorry, Mr Potter, I'd sooner take my chances in Glory. You're simply not my type.'

'You bitch!' Potter swore and raised a

hand as if to hit her round the face.

'Miss Watkins,' Cobb interrupted from behind.

Potter swung round, looked guilty and hurried away.

'What was all that about?'

'Nothing I couldn't handle but I think Mr Potter, as well as Miss Haynes, is going to find my presence disgusting from now on.'

'Never mind them. It isn't much further into Glory and then we can all say goodbye. Thank God!' They couldn't reach town fast enough for Cobb.

'I wonder why you agreed to do this for Marshal Hepworth when you so obviously consider it a waste of your valuable time.'

'Believe me, Miss Watkins, I wish I hadn't!'

'So do I. At least Marshal Hepworth is a gentleman.'

Bill and Dolly stood together at the gate waving them off and the coach began the last forty miles into Glory.

What with the heat, the rocking of the coach and the heavy meal they'd just eaten, everyone soon went to sleep. Potter leaned against poor Miss Haynes, Heather's head dipped towards Neil's bony shoulder and Cobb leaned, half in, half out of the window, in danger of losing his hat.

Knowing he was going to be in trouble for letting the coach be robbed, Groves tried his best to keep his eyes open but wasn't always successful and Jed Sykes held the reins loosely. The horses knew this stretch of country as well as he. He didn't need to give them direction. His head nodded against his chest. The horses, left to their own devices and knowing that the relay station wasn't far down the road, picked up speed.

It was then that the front wheel of the stagecoach hit a boulder in the road.

The coach bounced high up into the air...

Groves futilely yelled, 'Look out!'

...and came down with a thump that tumbled the passengers out of their seats.

'My God!' Cobb yelled while Heather caught hold of Neil and Miss Haynes rolled screaming on to the floor.

Sykes made an effort to pull on the reins of the suddenly scared horses but he was too late. The coach scraped along for a few yards and then slowly started to turn over. Groves was flung from the seat. The squeals and whinnies of the horses were matched by the screams and yells from inside the coach, and the high-pitched screeching of the wheels. The coach landed with a tremendous crash of breaking wood and snapping springs and skidded along the ground. The two rear horses fell under the wheels while the forward two come to a trembling halt caught up in the harness.

Everything went very quiet as the dust settled.

NINE

Groaning, Cobb tried to sit up and found he couldn't for the press of people above him. He was lying against the door that had come to rest on the ground.

110

The inside of the coach was quiet and still and he was scared that his fellow passengers were dead and here he was at the bottom of them all! Above him was a combination of Neil and Heather, one of her sharp-heeled shoes sticking in his ribs, while someone's elbow was uncomfortably jammed against his neck. Beyond that he could see a jumble of arms and legs. Then someone began to sob, making Cobb relieved that he wasn't the only one left alive.

Heather's foot wriggled away from him and then kicked him in the stomach. 'Keep still,' Cobb ordered. 'Mr Potter, are you all right?'

'I think so.'

'What about Miss Haynes?'

'She's fainted.'

'Can you get the door open?'

'I can try.' This was followed by more movement and cries of pain as the big rancher manoeuvred himself around to get at the door.

'This is awful,' Heather moaned at one point. 'I can't see anything.'

'Wait a minute and then you'll be able to get out,' Cobb told her.

Suddenly the door was opened from the outside, letting in welcome air and light, and Groves's voice said, 'You folks OK?'

'Get us out of here and I think we will be.'

Groves reached down for Potter's arm and managed to pull the man up and out. Together, with Neil pushing from behind, they lifted up the unconscious Miss Haynes. Still at the bottom, Cobb was buffeted by feet and arms as Neil and Heather got themselves sorted out and he suspected that maybe some of it was done deliberately. At last the weight of their bodies was off of him and he managed to clamber out by himself and jump down from the ruined coach on to firm ground.

He was a bit surprised to find that he was shaking and he hoped no one else would notice. It was unlikely for Heather had burst out crying and was being comforted by Neil, while Miss Haynes lay on the ground, eyes fluttering, tended by Potter.

Groves was unhurt, except for a cut over his eye and a sprained ankle.

Sykes hadn't been so lucky. Still holding the reins he had been tugged from the seat and trampled under the hooves of the rear horses, who, in their frightened panic, had kicked out, stamping into his body. He was still lying amongst the wreckage.

'Let's help him,' Groves said urgently.

Together he and Cobb cut loose the harness and lifted up the old man's body. He seemed very frail. They carried him over to the side of the road where some shade came from the rocky outcrop, and laid him carefully down. Sykes was still breathing, but barely. There was blood and bruising all over his face and his ribs had a caved-in look.

'He'll die if we don't get help,' Cobb said.

'I know. My God! What a mess.' Groves went back over to the stagecoach, picked up his rifle and making sure that none of the passengers was looking put the two rear horses out of their dying misery. There were tears in his eyes—for them, for poor

113

old Sykes and for himself. He went over to comfort the other two horses who were trembling violently.

The coach was ruined, lying on its side, one wheel in the air still slowly spinning, the other three smashed beyond repair.

Cobb went back to the passengers. Miss Haynes, whose black bonnet was sadly askew and crumpled, had now sat up. Potter had his arm about her shoulders. Heather had stopped crying but both she and Neil looked upset.

'What the hell happened?' Potter demanded. 'It wasn't anything to do with him and that bastard brother of his, was it?' he added, glaring over at Neil.

Cobb had momentarily wondered the same, but now he said, 'Of course not. Even if Travis didn't mind killing us just to rescue Neil he'd hardly risk killing him as well.'

'Gary wouldn't go to all that much trouble for me.'

'And if he did he'd have come galloping down here straightaway not waited till we got ourselves sorted out. No, it was just an accident. But it's left us stranded.'

'Exactly,' said Potter. 'So what the hell are we going to do now?'

'Take it easy,' Cobb said.

'Really, Mr Potter,' Miss Haynes pulled away from his sheltering arm, obviously quickly getting back to normal, 'your language is disgusting. I know we have been through an ordeal but there is no need to become so coarse. There are ladies present.'

'I'm sorry,' Potter said sheepishly, then turning to Cobb added: 'We must do something. I've a ranch to get back to.'

Cobb was getting tired of the man and his complaints. 'It's just as bad for everyone. Look at Sykes. At least you're not hurt.'

'Oh dear, poor Mr Sykes, is he badly hurt?' Miss Haynes struggled to her feet and went on shaky legs to the driver, bending down by him. 'Oh my! Oh my!' She went very white and looked as if she might faint again.

'Don't you worry,' Heather said. 'If Mr

Cobb frees me of these handcuffs I'll sit by him.'

'Will you dear?' Miss Haynes sounded very surprised as if never believing that a prostitute could have finer feelings.

'Yes. You rest and take it easy. You've had a bad shock. Will you let me loose, Mr Cobb?'

'I suppose it can't do any harm. There's not exactly anywhere you could go to around here.'

Potter interrupted. 'All this talk is all very well. But we can't stay here forever.'

From over by the horses, Groves said, 'The next relay station is about five miles down the road. I reckon the best thing is if I take a horse and ride there for help. It'll be quicker than going back to Bill and Dolly.'

'Yeah I guess,' Cobb agreed. 'Can you ride one of these horses?'

'It won't be easy. They're both still nervous and skittish and there's no saddle or bridle, but I'll have to, won't I? You folks should be all right here. It's hot and dry and I'll leave you what little water we had, though it ain't much. Just one canteen.'

'We'll have to manage.'

Groves took one last look at Sykes, patting his friend on the shoulder, then Cobb helped him up on to the horse he chose to ride.

'Good luck.'

'I'll be as quick as I can.'

Groves rode away at a trot. Once he'd disappeared beyond the rocks, Cobb sat down next to Neil. 'Might as well make ourselves as comfortable as possible,' he said, 'because now all we can do is wait.'

Groves wasn't really used to riding a horse, especially one where he had to stay on its back by clinging to its mane. Usually the trip into Glory was easy and uneventful. He couldn't believe all that had gone wrong this time. He was only glad that someone willing to take charge had been along. The passengers could be left in Mr Cobb's care without Groves having to worry about them.

The journey to the relay station seemed

to take forever but at long last he caught a glimpse of it through the trees.

'Thank God,' he breathed out loud, 'not long now.'

TEN

'Where the hell is he?' Cobb demanded, pacing up and down in impatience. 'He should have been back by now. He's been gone hours!'

'For goodness sake, Zac,' Heather complained, 'sit down. You're wearing me out.'

Cobb sat down, stood up, paced to where he could see further along the road, and then started back. He should have been the one to go for help. He couldn't abide sitting still, doing nothing; waiting. Waiting had to be about the worst thing in the world. But it had made sense for Groves to go. Groves was the one who knew the way and Cobb was the one who had two prisoners to keep an eye on. That didn't make it any easier.

He looked at the others. Heather had stayed by Sykes, holding his hand, comforting him when she thought that he could hear. Neil sat back against the ruined stagecoach, eyes closed, while Potter and Miss Haynes were by the side of the road. Miss Haynes didn't look very well and Cobb was scared that if help didn't arrive soon he'd have two sick people on his hands.

'I still say all this is something to do with that little bastard and his brother,' Potter growled, obviously itching for a fight. 'How else did that rock get in the road?'

Cobb ignored him. He went over to Heather, picking up the canteen of water. Only a splash was left in the bottom. She had been using it sparingly to wet Sykes's mouth, although he was unable to swallow. 'Just a mouthful,' he said to her.

'If we didn't let that little bastard have any there'd be more for us.' Potter took a swallow and passed the canteen on to Miss Haynes.

'It won't matter in a while. Groves is sure to bring us some more water and then we'll all have as much as we want.'

But Cobb was more worried than he sounded. Groves had been gone for far too long. Something was wrong. Supposing the horse had thrown him. Supposing no one was at the relay station when he got there. Supposing...well, supposing anything really. And here they were stuck out in the desert and needn't be found for hours.

He did a quick calculation. The stage would be expected at the relay station by now so even if Groves hadn't got there, then whoever was in charge might well come looking on his own initiative. If not, and Cobb wasn't any too sure about the initiative or otherwise of some stagecoach company employees, then the stage wouldn't be expected in Glory till early evening. Stagecoach itineraries being notoriously unreliable, no one would ask questions straightaway when it didn't arrive. It could be well on towards midnight before anyone realized something was wrong. By then it would be too dark for help to set out. So it would probably be morning before anyone decided to start a search, and then help had to get here. Perhaps he ought to take the other horse and ride back to the home station, seek help from Bill and Dolly.

'How far are we from Glory?' he asked Potter.

'About thirty miles.'

'I wish someone would come soon,' Miss Haynes said weakly. 'Supposing that young man's brother happens to come by. Then what will happen to us?'

'He won't rescue that bastard. I'll shoot him first.'

'Oh shut up,' Neil muttered. 'You weren't so brave when we were robbing you. You handed your money over easy enough.'

'You sonofabitch.' Potter lumbered to his feet and started towards Neil.

'Stop it!' Cobb intervened. 'Sit down. This bickering isn't helping anyone. And you be quiet too,' he added pointing a finger at Neil.

'Oh please, don't let's fight amongst

ourselves.' Miss Haynes burst out crying.

'Now see what you've done,' Potter accused Neil.

'It's not fair. You're all picking on me and I ain't done nothing.'

Cobb sighed. There didn't seem any way he could ride off and leave this lot on their own. God only knew what he'd find when he got back!

A few more endless minutes passed. Still no sign of the guard. This was stupid.

'I'm going up into the rocks,' Cobb announced. 'See if I can see anything.'

'Good.' Potter gave a smirk that Cobb didn't like.

The man was a coward and a bully. Everyone's tempers were on edge and while Potter was probably a law-abiding man normally, the circumstances weren't normal. In his frustrated impatience, he could just take it into his head to attack either Neil or Heather, or both of them. Cobb wouldn't be far away but even if Potter didn't have time to beat up Neil or rape Heather, he had a gun and it wouldn't take him long to use that.

'You two come with me.'

Neil got quickly to his feet. He feared much the same about Potter as Cobb and he intended to stick close to the lawman.

'What about Mr Sykes?' Heather asked.

'Miss Haynes can sit by him for a while. Come on.'

With Neil and Heather close behind him, Cobb climbed up through the rocks till he got almost to the top of the ridge and could see for miles down the stage road.

'Where do you think Mr Groves has got to?' Heather asked, sitting down and pushing her hair away from her face. 'What will happen to us if he doesn't come back?'

'Someone will come looking for us from Glory or tomorrow another stagecoach will come by. We'll be found sooner or later.'

'I don't want to stay out here all night not with that awful man watching my every move. He gives me the creeps.'

'Potter won't touch you, Miss Watkins.'

'What about me? It seems to me I'm the one he's watching.'

123

'Don't worry, kid, I won't let him touch you either. Not unless you deserve it.'

Neil scowled but said nothing. He turned his head away and at once saw a large dust cloud coming fast along the road.

'Someone's coming!'

'Oh thank God,' Heather cried.

'It can't just be Groves and the relay-station man, there's too much dust for that,' Cobb said. 'And they're coming at a mighty fast lick.'

'It doesn't matter who they are, Zac, it's help. Let's go down.'

They were halfway down the rocks when the riders reached the stagecoach. There were four of them. They were too far away for Cobb to make out what they looked like but for some reason all his training and instincts were alerted. He caught hold of Heather's arm. 'Wait!'

'What's the matter?'

'Get down.' Cobb pushed her down on the ground behind some rocks. 'You too,' he said to Neil and lying down behind a boulder, pulled out his revolver.

'What is it?' Heather repeated.

'I don't like the look of this.'

Below them the four men got off their horses, swaggering around as they took in the scene. Potter stood up and Miss Haynes left Sykes and came over to the rancher, standing close by him. They all spoke together and one man went to crouch by the injured driver. He came back, said something more to Potter and then hit the man hard round the face, knocking him to the ground. As Potter struggled to get to his feet, the man drew his gun and shot him.

'Christ!' said Cobb and beside him, he felt Heather jolt upwards in shock. He flung out an arm pulling her close to him, putting his hand over her mouth, stopping the scream that had arisen in her throat. 'Be quiet!' He glanced quickly at Neil. 'You too, kid. You make a sound, I'll shoot you.' Keeping Heather close to him, her head buried against his chest so that she couldn't see what was happening, he looked again at the men.

Miss Haynes had started to run towards the rocks, her arms flung out from her sides. The other men had their guns out now and they all fired, the sound of the shots reaching the watchers in the rocks a few moments later. Miss Haynes stopped as if she had reached an invisible wall, her feet seemed to get entangled one with the other and she tripped, falling inelegantly to the ground. A man went over to her kicking at her body.

'Oh my God,' Neil muttered.

That left the already dying Sykes. The first man went over to him again. They spoke and then calmly he shot the driver.

The four killers returned to their horses. They stared round, looking up at the rocks, at which Cobb and Neil ducked down, and then began to search the ground.

'They'll find our footprints,' Heather said, with something like panic in her voice.

'Not necessarily. The ground is pretty hard down there, and there was a lot of coming and going. Unless they've got a pretty good tracker with them, I doubt they'll be able to pick out our prints.'

'I hope they can't.'

It was soon clear that Cobb was right. The men stayed looking round for a while longer, had a short conflab, then got on their horses, riding away; as a last parting, they shot the remaining horse. They hadn't looked in the stagecoach or made any attempt to search the passengers' pockets. Robbery wasn't the motive.

'Stay here,' Cobb ordered and, leaving Heather in Neil's care, scrambled to the other side of the hill where he could make sure that the men had indeed gone. He waited until they had disappeared into the distance. When he got back Heather was shaking so much Cobb had to help her down through the rocks to the stagecoach.

'How could they?' she kept sobbing.

Potter and Miss Haynes were both as dead as Cobb had known they would be.

'Mr Cobb,' Neil called, 'Sykes is still alive.'

Cobb hurried over to the driver. There was blood all over his shirt from a bullet in his chest but his eyes were open. Cobb knelt down by him. 'Who were they? What did they want?'

Sykes clutched at his hand. 'Asking questions,' he croaked.

'Questions? What about?'

'Potter...said...nothing. Shot him.'

'What did they want?'

'Know about the passengers. Looking for...' His voice trailed away.

'Who?'

Sykes opened his mouth but this time only a bubbling sound emerged. His eyes glazed over and he loosened his grip on Cobb's hand, his arm falling back against the ground.

Cobb stood up, a bleak look on his face. 'So,' he said to Neil, 'they were looking for someone were they? You little bastard!' And without warning he launched himself at Neil, catching hold of his jacket collar and, shoving him back against the side of the wrecked stagecoach, shook him hard.

'You sonofabitch that was your brother looking for you! He killed all these people for you!'

'No!' Neil gasped, trying unsuccessfully to wriggle out of Cobb's grasp. 'It weren't him! He wouldn't bother. We always work alone. He ain't a killer!'

'Lying bastard!' Cobb said, and pushed Neil away so hard he fell over. 'Who else but you could they have been looking for? As he didn't find you here, your brother probably thinks you're still at the home station waiting for the stage back to Copper City and so that's where he's gone now.'

'Gary wouldn't go to all that trouble to rescue me. He's miles away by now. And where would those other men have come from?'

'They could have been waiting at your hideout.'

'Why don't you leave him alone?' Heather said, coming to stand in front of Cobb. 'You don't know what you're talking about.'

'Don't worry. I'm not going to touch

129

him again. He's not worth it. Judge and jury in Glory can decide on his punishment.'

'You're just taking it out on him because you didn't do anything to stop what happened.'

There was some truth in what Heather said. Cobb had witnessed the cold-blooded murder of three people and done nothing. Yet what could he have done? It had all happened so quickly. 'I don't have to defend myself to you,' he said but nevertheless he went on doing just that. 'There were four of them, one of me. I could never have got down here in time to prevent it.'

'You're meant to be a big-shot lawman. You could have done something!'

'And got us killed as well? I suppose that would have satisfied you?'

Heather knew that Cobb was right and, clutching her hands in front of her, she said in a much quieter tone, 'It's just so awful. Poor Miss Haynes. She'd been forced to come into this country and she didn't like it at all. And, poor thing, in the end she had every right to be scared.'

'I don't like it any better than you do. But right now there's nothing I can do about it. We've got to think of ourselves. So, we'd better see what we can find to take with us and then get out of here in case those men come back.'

'Aren't we going to bury these people? We can't just leave them like this!'

'I'm sorry, Miss Watkins, there doesn't seem to be much choice. It won't take Travis long to get to the home station, find the kid isn't there and then come back. And they won't hesitate to kill us because we're witnesses.'

'They're not looking for me,' Neil mumbled, but no one took any notice of him. He was very scared. It began to look as if he wasn't only going to be charged with robbery but being an accessory to cold-blooded murder as well.

Cobb got his saddle-bags from the boot of the stage. He took Potter's gun from its holster, made sure it was loaded and stuck it in his own belt. The canteen was

131

empty but he decided to take it along in case they came across a waterhole on the trail and could fill it up. Nothing else was likely to be of much help: no food, no more weapons—Groves had taken his rifle, Sykes's gun was an old-fashioned, single-shot revolver that would be of little use in a fight—no map. Still it was only five miles to the relay station. Hopefully they would find all they needed there. That was if they made it.

'Come here, kid.' He grabbed Neil's arm and released the handcuff from his right wrist. 'Miss Watkins, I know you don't like being shackled to him and I can't say I blame you but this way I can keep an eye on the pair of you. And you,' he poked Neil in the chest, 'if you so much as look in the wrong direction I'll knock you into next week. I don't take with innocent folks being gunned down, nor with those who associate with the sonsofbitches responsible. Just remember that.'

This time Neil didn't bother to protest. Cobb was unlikely to listen.

ELEVEN

Five miles didn't sound very far. On a horse it probably wouldn't have been very far. But Cobb had never had to walk that distance before and he soon realized exactly how far it was.

He had to keep to the stagecoach road, out in the open, because he didn't know the way otherwise. It was hot and dusty and with no water, his throat and mouth soon felt parched dry. His feet, cramped into his high-heeled, leather-tooled boots, quickly started to ache, he felt a blister come up on each heel. He didn't look back to see how Neil and Heather were getting on, he had enough to do to look after himself And always on his mind was the fear that the killers would come pounding up the trail behind them. Cobb was a good shot—fast and accurate—but he'd never be able to outgun four men.

After a couple of miles they entered the foothills that surrounded Glory. He wondered if he was anywhere near the trail he'd followed into Copper City but didn't think so, because as far as he knew, that went nowhere near the road. And he had no idea of how to get to it.

Pine trees gathered close providing some shade but at the same time the road got steeper and rockier, harder on the feet and legs. And in a way more dangerous because now Cobb couldn't see their backtrail.

'Can't we rest?' Heather asked. 'My feet hurt. This tight skirt and my shoes aren't meant for walking.'

'Nor are my boots.' Cobb peered ahead. 'It can't be far now,' he added with more hope than conviction.

Heather pulled a face but made no more complaint, trudging along by Neil's side. Neil looked as tired as Cobb felt and before long he was limping badly. But he didn't dare say anything, feeling sure Cobb would use any excuse to take his bad temper out on him.

It was getting dark by the time they

reached their destination. The road widened out into a meadow on the left-hand side and here the relay station had been built. There was room only for a small log house, a corral and tiny barn. A split-rail fence surrounded the property and separated it from the road. Smoke came from the chimney. Otherwise there was no sign of life and no horses in the corral either.

'It looks as if they did start out after us,' Cobb said. 'But for some reason never got there.'

'We didn't pass them on the way,' Heather pointed out. 'What do you think happened?'

'I don't know. Let's go inside. At least we should find water and food there.' The air was turning chilly and Cobb knew they couldn't go on much longer. It was pointless trying to travel during the night.

He led the way through the open gate and up to the house. Just as he was opening the door, Neil said, quietly, 'Over there.'

The body of Pete Groves hung over the

rail of the corral, a saddle by his side.

Despite the fact that he'd half been expecting something of the sort, Cobb swore under his breath. He drew his gun and went over to make sure the man was dead; he was.

'Come on and be careful.'

The door led into a windowless room that was so dark it was impossible to see beyond the small circle of evening light revealed by the open door.

Neil and Heather moved in behind him and almost at once Heather stumbled over something lying on the floor. It was the body of the relay-station owner. He, like Groves, had been shot. He'd managed to get his gun out but hadn't had the chance to use it.

'No wonder help never arrived,' Cobb said bitterly. 'Those murderers got here first.' What sort of men were they? These two hadn't stood a chance. They'd just been gunned down. And what for? Why kill them?

'What are we going to do?' Heather whispered. 'They could be back at any moment.' She flung a look at the door as if expecting the killers to be standing there.

'Kid, you look round, see if there's any food we can take with us. I noticed a well over by the corral, I'll fill the canteen.'

'Why the rush?' Heather asked. 'We can't make it to Glory tonight.'

'I don't intend to try. But we can't stay here.'

'Why not? It'd be shelter.'

'It didn't do this poor bastard much good.' Cobb poked the dead body with the toe of his boot. 'We've got to move on. Get away from the stage road. Our only chance lies in crossing the foothills.'

'But the road is where help from Glory will be,' Heather objected.

'No one will come now until morning. Potter said it was about thirty miles to Glory from where we had the accident. We've come another five miles. It's only fifteen miles back to the home station. Less than half the distance and half the time for those men.'

'We can't walk all that way, especially

through the hills, it's too far.'

'Will you tell me what else we can do? We have no choice. We're like sitting ducks if we wait here. Now, let's get a move on.'

'Oh you're impossible!'

Her frightened voice followed Cobb as he went outside and over to the well, beginning to wind the handle, bringing up the bucket. He liked this no better than Heather. Twenty-five miles still to Glory! And probably going through the foothills would make the distance even further because there would be no direct or easy route to take. On the other hand to wait here or remain on, or even near, the stagecoach road was to invite being found by the four killers. Maybe they weren't after rescuing Neil, maybe poor old Sykes had been wrong about the questions they were asking, maybe they were just random killers who were now in Copper City boasting about their exploits. Maybe. It was a chance he daren't take, when even now they might be on their way back here.

Not only that but he'd spent enough of the day doing nothing. He had to keep moving.

Neil and Heather came out of the house with another canteen, which Cobb also filled, and some cans of food and a can opener. They'd also found a couple of blankets. Somehow Cobb managed to stuff the food in his saddle-bags, giving Neil the canteens and blankets to carry.

'Hey, Mr Cobb, I suppose you wouldn't consider letting me have one of those guns?'

Cobb looked at Neil as if he was mad. 'You suppose goddamn right! What kind of a fool do you take me for?'

'I might need to defend myself.'

'Who against? They're on your side.'

Glad to get away from the open road, Cobb led the way into the trees. They hadn't gone very far when Heather said, 'How much farther are we going?' She looked and sounded bone tired, plodding on after Neil as if she couldn't take much more.

Cobb glanced back over his shoulder.

139

They were far enough in the trees for the road to have disappeared from view. Under their shelter it was now dark. 'Just a while longer. Make sure we're safe.'

It was about twenty minutes later when they came to an open spot that Cobb decided would make an ideal camp. It was surrounded by dense undergrowth through which they wouldn't easily be seen and which would make a noise to warn them of anyone's approach. And if the killers had any sense they wouldn't be riding through the forest in the dark but would also have made camp.

All three of them sat down in some relief. It seemed they had been walking for hours.

'It won't be so bad,' Cobb said. 'We've got food and water. We daren't risk a fire though in case it's seen. Here,' he passed Heather an open can of tomatoes.

She didn't eat much but Neil wolfed his share down as if he hadn't eaten for days. When they'd finished and had drunk their fill of water, Cobb said to Neil, 'Take the belt off your trousers.'

'What for?'

'Just do it.'

A sulky look on his face Neil took off his belt and handed it to Cobb. Zac then undid the handcuffs, shoved Neil back and handcuffed his wrists round the base of a pine tree. He then used the belt to tie Heather's hands together. He gave her one blanket and very reluctantly draped the other over Neil, leaving himself with just his coat.

'You don't believe in taking any chances do you?' Neil complained, as he tried to get comfortable.

'No. I'm also a light sleeper, don't forget that.' Cobb put a hand on his gun, turned over so that he was facing his two prisoners and closed his eyes.

'Oh please, Zac, can't we have a fire?' Heather asked after a while.

'No.'

'But it's so cold I'll never go to sleep.'

'It's not that cold but if you think it is then go and cuddle up with the kid. You'll have two blankets then.'

'Oh really, I'd rather freeze. I'd much sooner cuddle up with you.'

'I'm sure you would when I've got the guns and the handcuff keys and you think you'll get a chance to steal them while I'm asleep. No chance, Miss Watkins.' All the same as Cobb huddled down under his coat he wondered if he'd been too hasty in rejecting Heather's offer. It would be rather nice to snuggle up against a warm feminine body. He put all such thoughts from his mind. Duty first. Dammit.

And damn Glory! Damn Marshal Hepworth!

But then he was too tired to worry about the cold or anything else and he fell asleep.

Robin Bartlett sat in the old chair, glass of whiskey by his side, staring down at the bunkhouse, where a few lights still burned. He still couldn't figure out how or why things that were progressing so nicely had suddenly gone wrong.

As the moon came up over the trees his reflection looked back at him through the glass. He looked very serious but he'd faced worse problems in the past and always overcome them. He raised the glass to his lips and drank deeply.

TWELVE

'Will we get to Glory today?' Heather asked the following morning as they crossed the edge of an upland meadow.

'I don't know. I doubt it.' On foot Cobb wasn't sure what sort of progress they were making. If he'd been on horseback he would have had no trouble at all; as it was he didn't even know if they were going in the right direction, everything looked so different from the ground.

'It's very awkward being handcuffed,' the girl went on. 'Couldn't you trust at least me far enough to free me?'

'No.

'Can we rest a while?'

'Wait till we get amongst the trees.'

'Oh, why do you always have to have your own way?'

'Just trying to save all our lives.'

'Yes, so that Neil can go to jail and I can face the hangman. Thank you.'

Cobb took no notice. He was certain that the best way to handle the situation was to ignore everything but getting them back to Glory.

He was a few steps ahead of Heather and Neil and didn't see her as she glanced down at the ground. Putting a finger to her lips to warn a surprised Neil not to say anything, she pulled him over to one of the several dead treefalls amongst the pines. She picked up a fallen branch. It was heavy and solid.

'Quick!' she hissed at Neil running towards Cobb.

As they caught up with him, Zac turned round to see what was going on, and Heather swung the branch. It caught him round the side of his head and he fell to the ground, groaning, unmoving.

'What the hell did you do that for?' Neil demanded. Heather had acted too quickly for him to stop her and now he was horrified. 'You could have killed him.'

'Well I haven't. Come on, we've got to get away from him. He'll get us killed! Quick! Grab his saddle-bags!'

'We can't just leave him here.'

'Why not? He'll be all right. He's got a hard head. You don't want to go to Glory and be put in jail, do you?'

That made up Neil's mind for him. He most certainly didn't want to go to jail, especially as attacking a lawman and attempted escape would now be added to his crimes—for he had no doubt as to who would be blamed for this, and it wouldn't be Heather. And Cobb seemed to be breathing OK.

'If you're so worried we can leave him one of the canteens and a gun. But we'll take the blankets, we might need them.'

'All right. Quick, then.' Neil stuck Potter's gun in his own belt and grabbed up the saddle-bags. He flung the half-empty canteen down beside the unconscious detective. 'Let's go!'

Together they scrambled up amongst the

trees, zigzagging their way to the top of the hill. Once there, Neil looked back but could see no sign of pursuit. On the far side Heather stopped and sat down.

'What are you doing now?'

'You want to get rid of these, don't you?' Heather held up her handcuffed wrist. 'It'll be a lot easier then. The key is in one of the bags.'

Neil sat down beside her and opened the saddle-bags. He searched through them, then searched again.

'What's the matter?'

'It's not here.'

'It must be,' Heather screeched. 'I'm sure I saw him put it in there. Here, give them to me, you haven't looked properly.' She snatched the saddle-bags away from Neil, emptying them out on the ground. Both of them scrabbled about amongst the clothes and food. But Neil was right. There was no key.

'Oh, the bastard!' Heather exclaimed angrily. 'He must have had it in his pocket all the time. Oh!' Tears came into her eyes. 'Now what are we going to do? We'll have to go back and find it.'

'We can't. He'll have come to by now. He'll kill us.' Or, Neil thought, Cobb would kill him. 'It don't matter. We'll find something to break the chain with. We can make it like this, we have up till now.'

'I suppose so.' Heather didn't sound all that sure.

'What are we going to do?'

'What do you mean?'

'Well you do realize, don't you, that if we go to Glory, Mr Cobb will probably be there already waiting for us?'

Heather obviously hadn't realized that. 'We've got to go there. We can't go anywhere else. Not on foot. You must be good at evading the law, you'll just have to think of something.'

Neil was pleased at her faith in his abilities, although he had a feeling she was over-rating them and that she was much the cleverer. He touched her arm. 'Let's get on,' he urged. 'Cobb ain't gonna be very pleased when he wakes up. I don't wanna be anywhere around then.'

Neil was right about Cobb's mood. Slowly he'd blinked open his eyes, wondering for a moment why he was lying face down on the ground, before a pain threatened to split his head open. Groaning he put a hand to his forehead and felt a graze and some blood. He sat up, blinking several times and saw he was alone. At his feet was a canteen and a few tins. That was all. His saddle-bags had gone. And so had Neil and Heather.

Goddammit!

Slowly he hauled himself to his feet. Blackness threatened again for a moment but with an effort of will he overcame it.

Well if the pair of them thought they were going to get away with this, they were very much mistaken. Bellington's detectives weren't allowed to lose their prisoners. Picking up the canteen, Cobb put aside the pain in his head and set off resolutely in pursuit.

'Jesus Christ, what the hell is going on

here?' Marshal Hepworth pushed his hat to the back of his head, getting slowly off his horse. 'First those two dead bodies at the relay station and now these here! What the hell.'

Earlier that morning at the urging of the stagecoach company clerk, he and Tommy Reynolds had ridden out to discover what had happened to the stagecoach. Not really expecting any sort of trouble—there could be any number of reasons for its delay—Hepworth hadn't asked anyone else to go with them. Now he wished he had. Because trouble was surely what he'd found.

Tommy went over to the upturned stagecoach. 'It looks like there was an accident...'

'I can see that.' Hepworth's shock was making him short tempered.

'But they didn't die in it. They've all been shot! And, Marshal, here's Sykes, the driver, I recognize him.'

'God in heaven. What's going on?' Hepworth could only keep repeating his distress. 'Son, you'd better haul these bodies to the side of the road. I'll inform the stagecoach company of what's happened when we get back and they can send out a wagon to pick 'em up. Hopefully the office will also have their names and where they come from so any next of kin can be notified. But,' and the marshal found this the most puzzling part of all, 'there's still no sign of either Cobb or the girl.'

'It was this stagecoach they were on, wasn't it?'

'Yeah or meant to be anyway. But they ain't here.'

Tommy walked up and down and went a short way up into the rocks. He reported no sign of them. 'Perhaps they weren't on the coach after all.'

'They couldn't have been. Or, maybe for some reason, they stayed at Bill and Dolly's. Can't think why but Miss Watkins could've been taken ill I suppose. We'd better go and see.'

'Make sure Bill and Dolly ain't dead too.'

Hepworth hadn't thought of that. 'My

God I hope not! Come on, Tommy, let's get going.'

'For goodness sake, Cobb isn't coming after us,' Heather said in exasperation as, yet again, Neil looked back over his shoulder. 'And I'm not going to go down there and wade in that stream. I'm not getting my skirt all wet!'

Neil sighed. Usually he got on well with women. He liked them and they liked him. Heather was different. For a start she wasn't the usual kind of woman he knew. All right, she earned her living as a whore but not as one in a saloon; she was one man's mistress. That, as far as Neil went, almost made her like a proper wife and thus a good woman. And for another, most of the girls he knew were paid to show him a good time, to tell him how clever he was, to agree with whatever he said. While this talk was mostly lies, it was flattering all the same.

Heather had done nothing but argue and tell him he was a fool to take so many precautions. Her faith in his leadership hadn't lasted long.

She only wanted to get away. She didn't care about anything else. It was almost as if something beyond the fact that she was wanted for murder was urging her on.

'Yeah you are.' And Neil used his superior strength to drag her down the hillside to the stream that twisted and turned between rocks and trees through the valley at the bottom. He took no notice of her cries and struggles. 'If you're so worried you can take off your shoes and hitch up your skirt.'

'And show you my legs?' Heather glared at him. 'I'd rather get wet.'

'Please yourself.'

This high up in the hills the water was cold and Heather squealed as they waded into it and it went up past her knees.

'I don't know why we've got to do this,' she wailed.

'Because if Mr Cobb is following us we wanna put him off our trail. And those other men might be about.'

'Have you seen any sign of them?'

'Don't mean they ain't there. Now quit

moaning and come on.'

The stream was deep, fast running and had a bed of slippery stones. Once Heather fell over, going right under the water. She came up spluttering and coughing and very angry.

'If you so much as grin I'll...' Heather couldn't think of a bad enough punishment for Neil and her voice trailed away. She pushed her wet hair out of her eyes and wished that she'd stayed with Mr Cobb, stayed in Glory, and, in fact, had never left home and her parents.

After a mile or so, Neil pulled her up to the bank. Pointedly Heather tried to squeeze water out of her skirt.

'Now where?'

'Up I suppose.' Neil pointed at the hill looming over them. He didn't like to tell her how lost they were. That he had absolutely no idea of which way they should go. She was in enough of a panic and bad temper as it was and he was in enough trouble with her, without making it worse.

'More climbing?'

'Yeah.' At least if they got to the top they might be able to see something, some landmark that Heather would recognize. It was his only hope. Heather wasn't the only one wishing they hadn't escaped from Mr Cobb. Right then, even riding with Gary, with his impossible schemes and his ready blows, seemed preferable to wandering around the wilderness, shackled to a girl who thought him a fool, and whom he'd long ago decided he didn't like, not one bit, with no hope that things would get better.

'Come on let's go,' he said.

THIRTEEN

Cobb stared up at the sky. The sun was already low in the west. Night wasn't all that far away. He'd lost them. And not for the first time that day. Before he'd managed to find the trail again quickly. This time it might not be so easy for it was obvious they'd gone into the stream. It might take some while to find where they came out. The pair of fools, giving him the runaround like this. Just wait till he caught up with them, and he had no doubt whatsoever that he would catch up, he'd make sure they both regretted doing this to him.

'It'll be getting dark soon.' Neil looked up at the glimpses of sky through the tops of the trees. 'We'll have to stop for the night.'

'Yes and whose fault is that?'

'Mine I suppose. But you're the one who's meant to know this country, not me. I ain't never been to Glory before.'

'And who lost the blankets?'

'Me I guess. Look, Heather, arguing amongst ourselves ain't gonna change anything. We can't go on much longer, we'll lose our way for sure or risk having an accident.'

'I suppose you're right,' Heather agreed reluctantly. 'But don't go getting any ideas.'

'Ideas' were about the furthest thing

from Neil's mind. He was tired, his body ached and all he wanted to do was lie down and go to sleep.

'Look!' Heather came to a sudden halt and pointed.

Below in a slight gap between the trees on the hill they were crossing and those on the next was a farm.

In the gathering evening it didn't look much of a place. Just a tiny wooden shack, with a lean-to for a couple of horses next to it, and some pieces of equipment scattered about the yard. No fence, no smoke, no animals, no sign of life. It looked, and probably was, deserted, having belonged to a homesteader who thought he could make a living out here, then realized his error and left, the place rapidly returning to nature.

'We might find something down there to get rid of these dreadful handcuffs,' Heather said, her voice rising in hope. 'And somewhere to shelter for the night. Somewhere to dry off.' She still hadn't forgiven him for making her go in the stream.

Up close the farm looked as deserted as it had from a distance. Even so they tiptoed across the yard, just in case. But no one came out to challenge them.

'Look over there.' Heather pointed to a block of wood and a rusted axe near to the encroaching treeline. 'Perhaps we can use that. You do know how to use an axe, don't you?'

'Yeah, Miss Watkins, I do.' Neil sounded as if he was wondering whether it might not be a good idea to use it on her.

They went over to the block and laid their hands on either side of it, the handcuff chain spread taut between them. Neil picked up the axe and brought the blade down hard on the chain. The rusted blade promptly broke, leaving the chain intact.

'Oh for goodness sake. Can't you do anything right?'

While at the same time someone said from the direction of the trees. 'Looking for this?' And they both looked up to see Cobb standing there, holding the handcuff key.

'Oh shit,' Neil said and took a frightened step backwards.

'You stupid bastard! Leading me a dance like that!' And Cobb raised his hand to hit Neil.

'Stop it! Stop it!' Heather screamed, getting in between them. 'It wasn't his fault. It was mine. I was the one hit you. It was my idea.'

'In that case,' Cobb snarled, 'maybe I should hit you.' But all the same, he didn't.

'You're a bully,' she accused. 'Why don't you discover the truth before you lose your temper?'

Cobb ignored this. 'Why did you run away?'

'I was scared.'

'Well, for your information, Miss Watkins, all you've done is wasted most of a day. You've been going round in circles.'

'There I told you!' Heather flung angrily at Neil. Then suddenly crying out 'Get the key!' she launched herself in an attack on Cobb.

Neil had no choice but to go as well and

their combined weight forced Cobb to the ground.

For a while they all struggled together. Cobb was reluctant to hit Heather but she was scratching and biting and while he was busy with Neil, certainly not being reluctant to hit him, her fingers were scrabbling in his pocket for the key.

'Jesus Christ,' he muttered and slapped Heather hard on some soft portion of her body, hearing her squeal.

Neil rolled away and with a shaky hand drew out Potter's gun that was still in his belt. 'Give me the key or I'll shoot,' he said as everything came to a stop.

'All this is dreadful.' Bill sat at the table, his face ashen in the candlelight, while Dolly caught hold of his hand, holding it so tightly he almost winced. 'I can't believe it. Sykes and Groves dead! Shot! And the passengers too. They were only here yesterday. We were talking to them.'

'I'm sorry.' Hepworth was aware of the inadequacy of the words. 'And you're sure

Cobb and Miss Watkins left on the stage?'

'Oh yeah.' Bill nodded firmly. 'And Mr Cobb had another prisoner with him.'

'What's that?' Hepworth was startled. This was something he didn't know about.

'Yeah, some young kid who'd tried to rob the stage few miles back down the road. Him and his brother. His brother had gotten away with the proceeds and left the kid behind. The kid was caught by Cobb and Groves. Can you remember his name, Dolly?'

His wife shook her head numbly.

'Do you think that maybe it was his brother did all this to rescue him?' Tommy Reynolds asked.

'Can't think of any other explanation. But the kid seemed a bit of a sorry specimen to me, not the type to be involved in wholesale slaughter.'

'You can never tell,' said Hepworth.

'I felt a bit sorry for him,' Dolly added, but none of the men took any notice of this piece of female sentimentality.

'And you say that some other strangers came here?'

160

Bill nodded. 'That's right. Later on yesterday. Jed, that's the boy who looks after the horses, spotted 'em on the ridge. For some reason, I didn't like the look of 'em, although I don't know why, but you soon learn to be careful way out here. So we all came in here and barred the doors and windows. They rode down, pretending to be all friendly like and said they just wanted to ask some questions.'

'What kind of questions?'

'I don't know. I told 'em to clear off and sent a couple of shots out at 'em. They soon left.'

'Do you think they were the same men as killed Sykes and Groves?' Dolly asked, looking scared.

'Musta been. But who were they? What did they want? You didn't get a clear look at them, I suppose?'

'No, Marshal. It was getting dark by then and they didn't come up real close.'

'We could have been shot as well,' Dolly whispered.

Hepworth nodded. This was getting more and more puzzling. It didn't sound

161

like any normal sort of stagecoach robbery to him.

'Well if they were looking for the kid they obviously hadn't found him on the stage.' Bill said, and adding even more mystery to the puzzle, went on. 'So where is he and where are Mr Cobb and the girl?'

'That's what I'd like to know!'

FOURTEEN

'Oh, for Chrissakes,' Cobb said in disgust, taking little notice of the threat Neil posed. 'Give me the gun before it goes off and you hurt someone.'

'Give me the damn key.'

Cobb had no intention of doing that. If he couldn't handle someone like Neil Travis then he wasn't worthy of the name 'lawman'. He reached over, grabbing at Neil's arm and hand, catching hold of the gun and, at the same time, buffeting

162

him in the face with his elbow. To Heather's disgust, Neil gave up without too much of a fight, grabbing at his injured nose instead. 'That's better.' Cobb put the gun in his own belt.

'You idiot,' Heather hissed.

'Let's go inside, see what we can find,' Cobb said. 'And don't try anything foolish like that again, I might not be so lenient next time.'

They were halfway across the yard when a scrawny old man riding one scrawny old horse and leading a thin pony, appeared from the trees. He came to a halt as he saw them, then releasing the pony, slowly gigged the horse forward and idly holding a rifle in the crook of his arm, said, 'What you folks doing here, on foot an' all?' He quickly took in the fact that here was a lawman with two prisoners.

'It's a long story. We're meant to be on our way to Glory.'

'Then you're heading in the wrong direction,' the old man said with a chuckle.

163

'I know that. Unfortunately these two don't.'

'Well you won't get there tonight.' He got off his horse. 'Name's Dudley Shelton, by the way. You'd better come on in, have some grub, stay the night.'

'I don't want to put you to any trouble.'

'Won't be no trouble. There's stew to warm up. The kid there can sleep in the stable, got a good strong lock on the door, and the little missy can have the bed while you and me sleep on the floor.'

'OK then,' Cobb agreed, not particularly wanting to spend another night out in the open, and thinking it would be nice to eat something hot. 'Come on.' He shoved Neil and with hangdog looks he and Heather followed Cobb and the farmer into the shack.

It consisted of two rooms divided one from the other by a tatty curtain. When Shelton lit a couple of candles it was possible to see that dust and grime covered most surfaces and everything looked old and uncared for; it was obvious that housework didn't rate highly with the

164

man. But his stew was hot and plentiful, although Cobb didn't like to enquire too closely as to what might be in it.

'Here.' Shelton brought out some bottles of beer.

'None for them,' Cobb said.

'Why not?' Neil asked.

'You don't deserve it for trying to get away from me. You'll have to go without. If you're not careful I'll make you go without any food as well.' Cobb realized that the best way to threaten Neil was through his stomach.

'Been out here a long time,' Shelton said, as they all sat round the table. 'Just about scratch a living out of the ground. 'Course it was easier before all these ranchers started coming in, giving their orders, trying to drive the farmers away. I'm about far enough away from the flat lands they don't bother me much but several others have been forced to leave.'

'Don't you get lonely all by yourself?' Heather asked.

Shelton smiled, revealing almost toothless gums. 'I like my own company well enough. Get into Glory now and then. Get to meet people then.' He looked at Cobb. 'You say some men shot the passengers on the stage?'

'That's right.'

'Musta been awful. I wonder why.'

'They weren't robbers,' Cobb said. 'They were looking for someone.'

'Well it weren't anything to do with me,' Neil said quickly and mutinously.

'Don't know what things are coming to these days. Look at these two. Youngsters the pair of 'em, yet here you are hauling 'em off to jail. Coulda had a good life if they'd been willing to work hard. These days no one wants to work, let alone hard. They want an easy life. What you do, boy?'

'Tried to rob the stagecoach,' Neil said sulkily.

'Don't look much like a robber to me.'

'He's not a very successful one anyway.'

'And the little missy there. She doesn't look like she's done anything bad.'

'I haven't. It's all a mistake. But Mr

Cobb won't listen.'

'She's wanted in connection with a shooting in Glory. Mr Shelton, what direction do we take come morning?'

'Head east towards the sun. Glory's about fifteen miles. Doubt you'll make it in a day. It's pretty rough country.'

Cobb thought about asking the old man to accompany them, then decided against it. If those four killers were still out there it wasn't fair to put the innocent farmer at risk. Instead he said, 'You wouldn't have a couple of horses you could let us borrow, would you?'

The old man looked doubtful.

'I'd make sure you got them back. It would just make it a bit easier for us.'

'Well...I need one horse out here, wouldn't do to be left afoot, but you could take my old pony. Won't go very fast but the little missy there could ride it.'

'Thanks.'

When it was time for them all to go to sleep, Cobb led Neil out to the lean-to and pushed him inside.

'Pooh,' Neil said for it smelt powerfully of horses.

'I'm sure you've slept in worse places,' Cobb said and banged the door shut, locking it.

Neil had a moment or two of wondering if it was worth trying to escape. Deciding it wasn't he lay down in the few bits of filthy straw covering the floor, pulled his coat around him and tried to keep warm in the draughts that penetrated the slats of wood. At least he hadn't been expected to share the small place with a couple of horses.

'And you in here,' Cobb said to Heather, indicating Shelton's bedroom, which was beyond the curtain. The bed was lumpy with broken springs. 'Not exactly what you're used to. Nor is there anyone to share it with you. What a shame.'

'There's no need to be personal.'

Cobb chained her wrist to the bedpost and left her to get comfortable.

Not that he spent a very comfortable night either. He was used to sleeping, wrapped up in a blanket, on the floor; he wasn't used to having someone snoring fit to bust in his ear.

Still beggars couldn't be choosers and it was at least a roof over their heads. And at least in the morning Shelton cooked them bacon and beans and lent them his pony.

'I'll see you get him back as soon as possible,' Cobb promised. 'Thanks for all your help.'

'My pleasure. With luck you should be in Glory day after tomorrow.'

Cobb let Heather ride, her hands cuffed in front of her, while Neil's wrists were tied in front of him with a piece of rope borrowed from the farmer. He didn't expect trouble from either of them but this time he would be more than ready. It was his own carelessness that had allowed them to escape the day before; it wouldn't happen again.

Not that there seemed much chance of that as far as Neil was concerned anyway. He plodded along, the effort of putting one foot in front of the other seeming to be

169

as much as he could manage. And now, as they got ever closer to Glory, Heather too was quiet, her face white and set, as she thought about what fate awaited her there.

Cobb tried not to feel sorry for either of them. Their fate was no concern of his. They shouldn't have done wrong in the first place.

'Let's stop here for a while,' Cobb said. They'd come to an open glade amongst the pine trees, the sun shining on the tall grass and the splashes of colourful flowers. A small waterhole lay near to the edge of the glade beyond which a steep shale-covered slope led down to a narrow valley cutting through the hills.

Neil gave a sigh of relief and sank down on the ground, while Cobb helped Heather from the pony. She walked over to the waterhole, lay on her stomach and drank some of the clear cool water then lay on her back, staring up at the patch of sky visible above them.

Cobb also looked up. By his reckoning

there was still a couple of hours to go before it got dark. But maybe they should stay here, rather than attempt to go on. They'd had a hard day of it and they were all weary. Here at least was plenty of water.

Shelton had been right. They'd never make it into Glory in one day. They'd gone hardly any distance at all because Shelton was also right when he said that the going wouldn't be easy. There was no clear trail to follow and they'd had to cope with tangled underbrush, endless trees and rocky outcrops. A couple of times, mistaking the directions Shelton had given them, they'd reached a dead end and had to back track to find another way across the hills.

'We'll stay here the night,' he decided. He took hold of the canteens and went over to the waterhole, hunkering down to fill them up.

From the hills a shot sounded and a bullet ploughed up the earth beside him. Heather screamed in frightened shock and, as Cobb flung himself round, reaching for

171

his gun, an unseen voice yelled, 'Don't try anything stupid! We've got you in our sights.'

'Oh, God,' Neil said. 'It's them. They've found us.'

'Do something,' Heather urged frantically.

Another shot, a second bullet, closer this time. Cobb couldn't see the men. The men could see him and they could easily shoot him, the bullets had missed on purpose. Sighing in anger, and a certain amount of fear, he raised his arms, well away from his gun.

'What are you doing?' Heather cried.

'Put your gun down slowly,' the voice ordered. 'Carefully.'

'Don't!'

But Cobb did as he was told.

Then four men rode into the clearing.

'I hope you're satisfied,' Cobb said to Neil, but one look at his face and then at Heather's was enough to convince him of how wrong he'd been. It wasn't Neil that the killers were looking for, it was Heather. And they weren't likely to be friendly.

FIFTEEN

As the four men dismounted, Cobb recognised two of them. The one giving the orders was Dean Morrow, the foreman at the Circle B ranch, and another was Reeves, the bearded cowboy who had followed Cobb from Glory. The other two were also cowboys in their early twenties. So Robin Bartlett hadn't been content to let the law handle Heather Watkins. He'd sent his own men out to fetch her back. But surely he hadn't intended that they kill five innocent people in the process?

'Get up,' Morrow said to Neil, kicking him hard as he passed him. 'Get over with the other two.'

Neil did as he was told, standing on one side of Cobb, while Heather stood near to him on the other.

'Well, sweetheart, you sure as hell have given us the runaround,' Morrow said. He

173

went up to Heather and putting his hand under her chin, lifted her head so she was forced to look at him. 'Began to think we never would catch up. Robin will be pleased to see you.'

'You could pretend you didn't find us,' Heather said, desperation in her voice. 'I could make it worth your while.'

Morrow laughed. 'If Robin says so you'll make it worth our while anyway.'

'What I want to know is what you're doing chasing us like this, when I was bringing Miss Watkins back anyway.'

'You mean she ain't told you?'

'Told me what?'

'I would never have said anything,' Heather protested. 'Robin knows I wouldn't.'

'And why the hell did you find it necessary to kill all those people on the stage?'

Behind Morrow, the three young cowboys giggled together. 'You were on the coach then?'

'We were in the rocks watching. Why did you do it?'

'They might have recognized us,' Morrow

said in reply, but Cobb had a feeling it had more to do with enjoying killing for its own sake than anything else. The foreman poked his gun in Cobb's midriff. 'I'm getting fed up with all these goddamn questions.'

'Yeah, let's get on with it,' Reeves said excitedly.

'I should have shot you when I had the chance,' Cobb told him.

Reeves giggled. 'But you didn't!'

'No, but if I remember right you weren't so brave when you didn't have your friends with you.'

'Shut up!'

'What are you going to do, Dean?' Heather asked, her face white with fear.

'We're taking you back to Robin. He's the one got to decide what he wants done with you.'

'You can't,' Heather whispered.

'What are we going to do about the lawman?' Reeves asked.

Morrow stared at Cobb with a smirk.

'Let's kill him,' Reeves added.

'Not so fast.'

'What's the matter? Not getting a conscience are you? I'll do it if you don't want to.'

'It ain't that. I'm certain Robin will want the bastard killed but he'll want it done so that his body ain't never found or if it is it can't be connected to him. We'll take him back as well. Besides that way we can have some fun with 'em both. You'd like that wouldn't you? So, Mr Cobb, as you're the greater threat, you'd better be the one to wear the handcuffs.' Again he poked Zac with his gun.

Cobb reached into his pocket for the key, undid the handcuffs and gave them to Morrow. He squeezed Heather's hands in reassurance.

'Hands behind your back please.'

And Cobb was secured with his own handcuffs. He could hardly ever remember feeling so angry—or so scared—in his life.

'What about me?' Neil spoke for the first time since the men had come into the clearing.

'Yeah, who the hell are you anyway?'

'I ain't nothing to do with them. Look,'

Neil held out his own trussed-up hands. 'He was taking me in as well. You can let me go. I ain't your enemy. I won't say anything. Honest.'

'Hmm,' Morrow looked at him. 'You don't say?'

'Yeah, I do. Him and the girl mean nothing to me.'

'He's right. He's just a thief I arrested along the way. Let him go; all he'll do is get out of the country as fast as he can.'

'I'm inclined to believe you both. Trouble is you might not be telling the truth.'

'We can't take all three of 'em back to the ranch,' Reeves objected.

'I know. But as there's absolutely nothing to connect the little bastard to us, it won't matter if his body is found.' And raising his gun, Morrow shot Neil.

'Jesus Christ!' Cobb exclaimed as Heather screamed, covering her ears with her hands.

The force of the bullet at such close range caused Neil to skitter backwards. His feet tripped over the waterhole and, legs flailing, he slipped over the edge of the slope and slid quickly and awkwardly down through the shale to land, unmoving, at the bottom.

'How could you!' Heather cried. She tried to hit out at Morrow but the man held her off easily.

'I ain't any too sure he's dead,' Reeves said, peering over the edge at Neil's body which lay far below.

'Don't matter much,' Morrow callously replied. 'If he ain't now he soon will be. Let's go.'

'You sonofabitch,' Cobb said.

Morrow laughed. 'I should be quiet iffen I was you or by God when we get back to the ranch you'll find out just what sort of a sonofabitch I can be. You and the girl both.'

Reeves giggled and now that Cobb was safely handcuffed and couldn't do anything, he hit out at the lawman. While Morrow watched indulgently, the other two cowboys joined Reeves and for a few moments, all three punched and kicked Cobb to the ground.

'Oh, stop them!' Heather said, catching at Morrow's arm.

The man took no notice; he was enjoying this almost as much as the others. It was only when Cobb was lying helpless and receiving several kicks in the ribs, that he said, 'OK that's enough for now. Let's get back to the ranch.'

A bit disappointed, Reeves nevertheless pulled Cobb up and shoved him towards the horses.

'Come on, sweetheart,' Morrow said to Heather, 'you can ride in front of me. Reeves, Laurence, you ride either side of Mr Cobb. He tries any tricks you can beat him up some more. But don't kill him. I want that pleasure myself.'

Cobb somehow managed to stay on the back of the horse. His face and body ached and there was a dull pain in his ribs which he rather feared might be broken. Blood dripped from a cut over his left eye. He didn't understand anything of what was going on, except that it must have something to do with the death of Norman Tomlin, which obviously wasn't as clear cut as he and Marshal Hepworth had thought.

If he'd had his mind more on the job and not so much on going to St Louis he might have worked that out earlier. He certainly might have worked out that Heather was so scared because she knew she was the one the men were looking for and they were nothing to do with poor Neil.

But it was too late for might have beens.

Now he had to think of a way out of this mess. And that wasn't going to be easy.

These men were killers, working on the orders of their boss. If Heather could convince Bartlett that she would keep quiet about whatever it was she'd done or knew, she might not be killed, although he didn't like to think about what else they had in mind for her. He obviously would have to be shot—they would know he couldn't and wouldn't keep quiet about the killings he had witnessed—and before it happened Morrow and his men were going to beat the living bejesus out of him.

By cutting across country it wasn't far to the Circle B ranch. They reached it just as it was getting dark. The only lights shone from the bunkhouse, the rest of the place was quiet.

'Looks like Robin is out somewhere,' Morrow said. 'Let's lock these two up for the night and leave 'em to think about their fates.'

They rode up to the house from the rear where they couldn't be seen from the bunkhouse. That meant Morrow didn't want the other hands to know what he was up to. Cobb digested the information, thinking it could prove useful, although he didn't know how at the moment. He was pulled roughly from the horse. With a gun stuck in his side and told to keep quiet, he was marched through the back door. Morrow was close behind him leading Heather.

'Upstairs.'

They were shoved into a bedroom.

'Sweet dreams,' Reeves mocked.

The door was shut and locked behind them. It was dark in the room, a sliver of light coming from between the shutters that secured the one window.

As soon as they were alone Heather flung herself at Cobb, putting her arms round his neck, crying. 'Oh, Zac, I'm so frightened,' she managed to say between sobs. 'They're going to kill us.'

'Not if I can do anything to stop 'em,' Cobb replied.

'How can you do that? You've no gun and you're handcuffed.'

'Well, if you put your hand in my trousers' back pocket you won't find a gun but you will find a spare key for the handcuffs.'

Gulping back her tears, Heather did as she was told and soon Cobb's hands were free.

'That's better.' He flexed his wrists and arms.

'At least now you know how much they hurt,' Heather said. But her little spurt of temper quickly died and she slumped on the bed, looking defeated.

Cobb tried the door and the shutters. They were all securely locked. And Morrow must have put a guard outside. They were trapped. He went over to the bed, sat beside Heather, took hold of her shoulders and gave her a little shake.

'I think you owe me some sort of explanation,' he said.

SIXTEEN

'You knew who those men were all along, didn't you?' Heather gave a little nod. 'And that they were after you?'

'Yes, of course. I was so scared after they killed all those people. I knew they would kill me too. Zac, do you think Neil is dead?'

Cobb's face turned bleak. 'It looks that way. He was shot in the chest. Anyway that bastard, Morrow, is right. If Neil isn't dead now, a night out in the cold, badly wounded, nowhere to go, he soon will be. Come on, Heather, tell me what's going on.'

'Marshal Hepworth was partly right. I was Robin Bartlett's mistress. And Norman Tomlin was shot. But I didn't shoot him.'

'So, what happened?'

Heather pulled away from Cobb, sitting on the bed, back up against the pillows, arms round her knees. 'At first I thought I loved Robin and that he loved me. I arrived in Glory with nothing. I was resigned to getting a job in a saloon or a brothel. I'd worked in saloons before and I didn't much like the idea but I didn't see what else I could do. Then I met Robin. He set me up in my own lovely little house in town and made me promise I would entertain only him. It was an easy promise to make.'

'Why didn't he have you living out here? Marry you?'

'I don't know. Maybe it was because it wouldn't look good. Although Robin had never been particularly ambitious and as far as I know there's no respectable girl in Glory he's got his eye on. Besides, everyone knew I was his mistress. Perhaps he didn't really love me. Perhaps he just wanted me for the time being. It didn't really matter. He was handsome, easy going, kind; or so I thought.'

'You found out he wasn't?'

'One day Dean Morrow saw me talking to a young cowboy. I told Robin there was nothing in it. We were just talking. It made no difference. He had the cowboy beaten up and he hit me too.'

'Why did you stay with him?'

'Because afterwards he begged my forgiveness and said it was only because he loved me so much.'

'And you believed him?'

'Not really. But while he can be very cruel he can also be very generous. And if I'm honest I knew that nowhere else would I have my own house or so much money of my own to spend. Also by then I was frightened of him. I didn't dare leave him.'

'And what about Tomlin? Did he want you as well?'

'Of course not. Norman was God-fearing and strict. He disapproved of Robin having a mistress and he disapproved of me and what I did. He more or less ignored me whenever we met. Then he became Robin's partner. I don't know why, they were completely different. But he had money he wanted to spend and Robin wanted money to spend and Robin is charming when he wants to be and so I suppose he charmed Norman.

'Anyway Norman must have discovered that while he was putting money into the ranch for certain improvements, and therefore profits, to be made, the only improvements were those that benefited Robin, like this house. That was what the quarrel was about, money.'

Cobb was figuring things out for himself. 'Bartlett or one of his men killed Tomlin when he was here that day?'

'It was Robin. Oh, Zac, it was awful, he just shot him down, like Morrow did with Neil. Robin didn't expect Norman. He never had me here if Norman was about because Norman made a fuss. We'd just made love when he arrived. Robin told me to stay in the bedroom. As I was dressing they started arguing.'

'How did you know the fight was about money?'

'I heard most of it. Norman was shouting. I'd never heard him raise his voice before so I was curious and listened to what they were saying. Norman wanted to go to the bank and get all of his investment back. Robin was telling him not to be so stupid. By this time I'd crept to the bottom of the stairs.' Heather closed her eyes for the moment. 'Robin pulled out his gun and shot him. Just like that. Norman never carried a gun, only a rifle in the saddle scabbard, which naturally he hadn't brought into the house. He was unarmed. He didn't stand a chance.' She stopped, putting her hands over her eyes as if she could shut out the scene.

Cobb patted her shoulder.

'Robin looked up and saw me. He smiled. But I'd seen the look he gave me first. He would kill me rather than risk having me give him away. I panicked. I should have stayed, assured him I wouldn't say anything, and then gone home, got my

187

things and some money and left.'

'He might not have let you.'

'Perhaps not. It doesn't matter now. I ran. My action must have taken him by surprise because I'd always done what he wanted before. I managed to get to my horse and took off on it. Some men, Reeves and Forrest I think, pursued me but I was amongst the trees and somehow I lost them. I didn't dare go back to Glory, Robin would have had someone waiting for me there, so I rode to Copper City. I should have carried on going. But I was frightened, I had no money, I didn't know what to do.'

'And in the meantime Bartlett and perhaps Morrow as well waited till it was dark, then they took Tomlin's body back to Glory, left it in your bed, fired a shot and made out you'd killed and robbed him.'

'Robin had to dispose of the body, he had to find a scapegoat for the shooting, so why not me? And if I was caught it would make my story hard to believe. Especially as I'm sure he would have plenty of witnesses to give him an alibi.'

'It would also ensure that the marshal did his best to get you back and so allow Bartlett to try to get to you first. What I can't understand is why Morrow killed all those people. Surely Bartlett won't like that.'

'You have to understand them, Zac. Robin and Dean have known each other for years. They both started out as rustlers working for a gang, when I'm sure life was cheap, until Robin decided he could make more money working for himself. So he stole the cattle from the rustlers he was with and sold them at a profit. There was some kind of shoot-out where he and Dean came out best. Then, together with Dean, he headed here, founded the Circle B, rustled more cows and became reasonably respectable. Morrow stayed on as his foreman. From what Robin has said when he's drunk they weren't slow to shoot and kill in the old days and obviously when things go wrong they're not slow to solve their problems that way now.'

'Hepworth said some of Bartlett's men

caused trouble round Glory but it was never bad enough to do anything except make them spend a night or two in jail.'

'Bartlett does have a few ordinary cowhands working for him. The three who were with Dean—Reeves, Laurence and Forrest—are all hell-raisers. They do work hard but they also like to play hard. While they haven't caused any real trouble in Glory, trouble has been caused elsewhere and I know for a fact that Reeves has killed a couple of men in gunfights. Still, I didn't think Dean was capable of cold-blooded murder.'

'Heather, why didn't you tell me this before?'

'Because I was scared and I didn't think you'd believe me. Why should you? And you were so stern and cold.'

'Was I?'

'Yes. You frightened me. And you terrified poor Neil.'

'Did I?'

'And you were taking me back to Glory where Robin was. That's why I tried to get away from you. I didn't hurt you did I?'

190

Heather reached up, touching Cobb's head where she'd hit him. She sighed. 'It doesn't matter now. They're going to kill us.'

'I told you not if I can help it.' But Cobb didn't know what he could do. He was unarmed, facing up to overwhelming odds. Even a Bellington's private detective had limits.

'Here, son, have some water.'

Neil groaned as strong arms helped him to sit up. His whole body felt like it was on fire. For a dazed moment he couldn't think where he was or what had happened. Then he remembered. He'd been shot. The memory of the moment of unbelieving fright flashed through his mind. The numbing pain as the bullet struck him, knocking him backwards, the terrifying slide down the slope; slipping into unconsciousness.

He didn't know how long he'd been lying here. He was suddenly scared. Was this one of the men come to finish him off? He didn't really think it could be, not when he was being held gently and he was being given cold water to drink.

He stared up at the man helping him. It was the old farmer, Shelton.

'Lucky for you I heard the shots and came to see what was happening,' Shelton said. He laid Neil back down and pushed open his jacket revealing the wound that had torn a hole in his side. 'It weren't that Mr Cobb did this to you were it?'

'No. It was the men he told you about. They knew Heather. They shot me. Am I going to die?' It surely felt like he was.

Shelton chuckled. 'Shouldn't think so, son. The bullet's gone straight through and hasn't hit anything vital. There's a helluva lot of blood but it seems to have stopped now. Let me wrap it up. Probably ache like hell.'

Neil's shirt was torn to become a makeshift bandage, which the old man wrapped round his chest and back and tied tightly.

'Where are Mr Cobb and the little missy?'

'The men must have them.'

'Do you know who they were?'

192

Neil thought hard. 'One of them mentioned someone called Robin.'

'Ah yes, Robin Bartlett. He owns the Circle B. Bartlett is one of those newcomers who delight in chasing the original farmers out. He's a real mean bastard when he thinks no one is looking. You know what he wants with 'em?'

'No. How far is the ranch?'

''Bout a couple of hours away.'

'Help me up.' Neil got to his feet. 'Ouch!'

'You OK, son?'

'I will be.'

'You'd better come back with me and rest a while.'

'All right.' Neil was glad of the man's support. He'd never been shot before. He felt sick.

Cobb and Heather sat on the edge of the bed holding hands, talking in whispers about how they might escape. So far no solution had been found. Suddenly the door opened and Cobb just had time to put his arms behind his back pretending to still be handcuffed before Robin Bartlett stepped inside. He held a gun and behind him stood Morrow also with a gun in his hand. Bartlett grinned as Heather tried to hide herself behind Cobb.

'My, my, isn't this cosy? The two of you snuggling up together. Are you sure your Mr Bellington would approve?' Bartlett's voice turned nasty. 'You know for a while I was scared that maybe you would make it back to Glory. I wonder who our good marshal would have believed, you or me? Still don't matter now does it? You ain't going to get a chance to tell anyone your story.'

'There's no need to kill Heather,' Cobb said quickly. 'She won't say anything to anyone.'

'You mean my dear Heather would be willing to face the hangman for me, when she knows I deliberately set her up?' Bartlett laughed. 'Don't be so goddamned stupid, Mr Cobb! And don't be so much of a gentleman. I ain't one and Heather isn't used to anyone with manners. I'm afraid I'm left with no choice but to have you

194

both killed. I don't care about you, Cobb, you're a lawman you know you have to take your chances. I am sorry it's come to this for Heather. I did love you, you know, but you should never have run out on me. We could have worked something out.'

'Oh be quiet,' Heather said with a spurt of defiance. 'Anyway, Robin dear, I never loved you, you were just a convenient meal ticket!'

For a moment Cobb thought Bartlett was going to strike the girl, then he laughed again. 'My poor Heather. I wonder if you'll be so fiery tomorrow when you're taken well away from the ranch and my men have their wicked way with you. I shan't be here by the way. I shall be establishing an alibi should it be needed in Glory. Well, dear, night-night, pleasant dreams.'

And the door was banged shut.

'Oh, Zac,' Heather said and crept into the shelter of Cobb's arms.

'Don't worry, sweetheart, don't be scared.'

'Aren't you scared?'

Cobb felt there was no point in lying.

Heather wasn't stupid. 'Yes, I suppose I am.'

For a while they sat and held one another. Then Heather raised her face to his and gently kissed him.

'This isn't to get your own back on Bartlett is it?'

'Oh no, Zac, no.'

And suddenly Cobb wanted the comfort and caring of her body. He pushed her back down on the bed and began to undress her.

'Zac,' she whispered.

And for a time they forgot their troubles in each other's arms and each other's kisses.

SEVENTEEN

Robin Bartlett sat for most of the morning in the saloon, drinking. Because he had money, and was normally generous with it, a crowd of hangers-on usually gathered round. Today no one came near. Everyone could see he was in a foul mood and unpredictable with it.

Bartlett was trying to drown his sorrows and not succeeding. His mind was on the events at the Circle B. He couldn't have cared less about Cobb, but in his own selfish way he loved Heather Watkins. Yet he could see no alternative to having her killed. She had witnessed him shooting an unarmed man and, however much she protested to the contrary, would either have told the law or blackmailed him into giving her even more than he had already.

And the worst of all, she had actually run out on him, dared to leave him. What Bartlett had he owned and it was his until he said otherwise.

He was aware that everyone in the saloon was muttering about his strange, ugly behaviour. He had to be careful. He didn't want to arouse any suspicions. After all there were plenty of other whores who'd be more than willing to become his mistress. Heather was one among many.

He'd go along to the general store, order some things for the ranch, behave normally. But first perhaps he'd have just one more drink.

It was mid-morning. Cobb, with Heather behind him, faced the foreman, Morrow, and the three other men—Reeves, Laurence and Forrest. Much earlier Robin Bartlett had ridden away and Morrow had then waited until the rest of the men, the ordinary cowboys, had left the ranch headquarters for the day. Now he and the others had all the time in the world to do whatever they wanted, and without anyone to try and stop them, or even to know.

Cobb had his arms behind him, the handcuffs round his wrists but not secured. He hoped no one would check up on them. It was his one advantage. Admittedly a small one but at least it might give him an element of surprise.

'Come on, let's go.' Morrow pulled Heather away from Cobb, dragging her out of the room after him. 'I'm having first go, boys, then she's all yours. And you can watch, Mr Lawman.'

The other three laughed, nudging and poking Cobb as they accompanied him down the stairs to the rear door, outside of which five horses were tied up.

'Where are you taking us?'

'To some nice spot where we won't be disturbed,' Reeves grinned.

They all went out on the unfinished porch and, at the same moment, Neil stepped out from round the side of the house. He carried Shelton's rifle and shot at Reeves, who was nearest to him.

Neil wasn't a very good shot. He missed. But it provided a diversion. Ducking out of the way, Reeves fell off the porch amongst the hooves of the horses. The animals began to whinny in fright, jerking this way and that in their effort to get away. With a yell, Reeves rolled out from under them and into the open. At the same time, Forrest and Laurence both went into a crouch, pulling out their guns, firing back at Neil.

Cobb freed himself of the handcuffs, flinging them at Laurence, hitting him in the face, putting him off his aim. He yelled. 'The rifle!'

Neil flung it at him. Cobb caught it and in one fluid movement, swivelled round and shot Forrest. The man's arms flew out from his sides, the gun slipping from his slackening grasp, and he tumbled backwards, landing on his side and not moving again.

Meanwhile Heather kicked out at Morrow and tried to get away from him but he grabbed her round the waist, pulling her back inside the house.

Neil ran in a crouch to where Forrest's gun lay on the ground. As he picked it up, Reeves fired at him. The bullet whined past Neil's ear and Neil fell over on to his back as Reeves came towards him, aiming again. Half sitting up, Neil raised the gun in two shaky hands and sent several shots towards the man. That close even Neil couldn't miss and one of the bullets took off the top of Reeves' head. For a moment he remained standing, a surprised look in his eyes, before collapsing on to the ground.

Cobb and Laurence had exchanged several shots, each of them missing as they ducked and dived out of the way. But now Laurence had two weapons lined up on him and with a cry of fright he flung his gun down and put up his hands.

'Hold it right there, all of you,' Morrow said from behind Cobb.

Swinging round Zac saw the foreman standing in the doorway, his arm round Heather's neck, revolver barrel dug into her side. 'Let her go.'

'I ain't that stupid. Put down the goddamned guns the pair of you. Laurence pick 'em up and come over here.'

'What are we going to do?' Laurence whined as he took the gun from Neil's hand. 'Reeves and Forrest are dead.'

'Shut up,' Morrow growled. 'All we gotta do is kill all three of 'em here and goddamned now!' And he raised the revolver from Heather's side and pointed it at Cobb.

Heather screamed and stamped her foot down hard on Morrow's instep. With a cry of sudden pain, he relaxed his hold and Heather squirmed out of his grasp. Morrow was left undecided as to whether to shoot at Cobb or try to catch hold of the girl again.

Cobb wasn't undecided at all. He swung round, punched Laurence hard on the nose, breaking it in a spray of blood and bone, sending the young man stumbling backwards. Cobb then flung himself forward to snatch up the rifle. On one knee he shot upwards and the bullet caught Morrow in the throat. The man grabbed at the wound, as if that could stop the flow of blood, staggered a little and was dead before he fell.

'Zac!' Heather cried and ran up to him. 'Zac!'

They clung to one another and over her shoulder Cobb looked round at the scene. Neil was once more holding a revolver, pointing it at Laurence who had clearly lost all desire for a fight. The other three were dead. Gradually the horses quietened down and the wisps of gun-smoke drifted away.

'Christ almighty, Mr Cobb,' Neil said shakily. And he walked away, falling to his knees.

After a while Cobb put the still trembling Heather away from him and went over to Neil. 'You OK?'

'I ain't never shot anyone before.'

'It needed doing. It was either them or us. And you know what they would have done to Heather before they killed her.' He helped the young man to his feet. 'Where the hell did you spring from? We thought you were dead.'

'Shelton helped me. He bandaged me up, lent me his rifle and his other horse and told me where they'd taken you.'

'Well, thanks.' Cobb was aware that the words were inadequate but it was about all he could think of to say.

'It's all right,' Neil said with a little smile.

'We'd better get out of here before Bartlett or any of the other cowboys get back. Someone might have heard the shooting and be coming to investigate.'

'What are we going to do about him?'

Neil asked, nodding towards the frightened, sulky Laurence.

'I'd like to take him into Glory but my main concern is to get us all there, safely. So I'll lock him up, see how he likes it. Come on, you, inside!' When he came back Neil and Heather were talking together, anxious looks on their faces. He had no doubt that they were talking about him and what he was going to do with both of them. Heather's innocence was, of course, proved beyond doubt, but Neil was still wanted for the stagecoach robbery.

Neil stepped away from Heather, and said, belligerently. 'Why should I come with you?'

He still had the gun and Cobb felt too tired to do anything if Neil decided to make a break for it. It certainly wasn't worth another shoot-out. 'Because I think you'd be better off with me than out there on your own. Morrow and the others might have been bastards but I don't suppose the rest of the hands know that. They won't take kindly to what's been done out here.

And you'd better get that wound seen to properly.'

'Am I still under arrest?'

'Yes.'

'Oh!' Heather exclaimed indignantly. 'How can you be so mean? Neil helped us. He saved our lives. He had no reason whatsoever to come back and risk his own life for us. Yet he did and he saved us too. We'd be dead without his help. And he's not a bad person, he hasn't done anything really wrong.'

'It's not Mr Bellington's policy to let any outlaw go, whatever he has or hasn't done.'

Heather muttered something very rude about Mr Bellington's policy.

'It's all right, Heather,' Neil said. He handed over the gun to Cobb, who stuck it in his belt. 'I know I've done wrong and have got to pay for it.' He sounded very unhappy.

Aware of Heather's scowl boring into his back, Cobb went over to the waiting horses. 'We'll take three of these. We'll be back in Glory in a couple of hours.'

EIGHTEEN

Marshal Hepworth was a very worried man. Where were Cobb and Miss Watkins? Were they dead? Was their disappearance something to do with the young thief, or with the mysterious killers? And who were the killers? What did they want besides killing people? He was beginning to think he'd have to wire Mr Bellington about the disappearance of his detective. And that would surely mean more trouble.

And now Robin Bartlett was in town, getting pretty likkered up by the looks of things, making a nuisance of himself over at the store. Well Bartlett's behaviour was one thing he could deal with.

Hepworth wandered over to the door and stepped out. Tommy Reynolds was hurrying towards him and as he saw the marshal he pointed down the road. Hepworth followed his gaze. And straightened.

It was Zac Cobb, Heather and another young man, who was leaning tiredly forward over the saddle pommel. Cobb certainly didn't look like the neat young man who'd left Glory a few days ago and Hepworth had never seen Heather so dirty and untidy. What the hell had been going on?

'Come with me,' he said to Reynolds as the young deputy reached him. 'There are some questions to be answered!'

At the same time from across the road, Robin Bartlett came out of the store on to the sidewalk. He too saw the approaching riders and stiffened in shock.

'Nearly there,' Cobb said. 'You feeling OK?' he added to Neil.

'Yeah I guess so.'

Suddenly from ahead of them there was a disturbance amongst the citizens who were shopping or gossiping. There were a few cries and yells and people moved quickly, leaving a gap in which stood Robin Bartlett, gun in hand, pointed at them.

'Look out!' Heather screamed a warning.

But before anyone could do anything, Bartlett fired. The bullet hit Cobb's horse which reared in pain. Although taken by surprise, Cobb managed to cling to the animal's neck but the horse fell backwards, taking Cobb with it. As he hit the ground the horse rolled on top of him. He was trapped.

More bullets from Bartlett's gun had followed the first.

'Get off!' Neil yelled and he and Heather flung themselves off their horses. Neil scuttled towards the nearest sidewalk and what shelter he could find, but Heather had to crouch in the middle of the road with nowhere to go.

All round men and women yelled and screamed, as they didn't wait to find out what was happening but prudently dived for cover. A loose horse galloped by, almost knocking Heather over.

'What the hell is this?' Hepworth growled. He didn't like shoot-outs in his town, especially when he didn't understand them. 'Bartlett!'

But, reloading his gun, the rancher took

no notice. He was too angry and scared to take any notice of anything. Maybe if he hadn't been so drunk he wouldn't have done what he did. As it was all he wanted to do was kill the lawman and the bitch so that they couldn't tell tales; and to avenge Dean Morrow for, the fact that they were here in town must mean that somehow Cobb had killed Morrow and the others. Goddammit he and Dean had been friends.

How he would explain his shooting Cobb and Heather he neither knew nor cared.

Helpless, Cobb lay under the dead horse, watching Bartlett, still firing at Neil, keeping him pinned down, stalk towards him and Heather. Frantically he tried to reach his gun. Somehow he managed to squirm his body round far enough to get it out of the holster. Before he could do anything else Bartlett was beside him, kicking the gun out of his hand.

'You bastard!' Bartlett yelled and holding his revolver in both hands he pointed the barrel at Cobb's forehead.

'God,' Zac whispered, not sure whether he was swearing or praying. He shut his eyes.

'Bartlett!' Hepworth yelled again. 'Out of the way! Out of the way!' With Tommy Reynolds close behind, he was racing towards the confrontation, unable to do anything. He didn't dare fire because of the townspeople in his way. He was going to be too late to stop the rancher committing murder.

Bartlett squeezed back the trigger.

'Oh no, you don't!' Heather dived for Cobb's gun.

Cobb heard the sound of a shot. Much to his surprise there was no pain. He opened his eyes. And saw Bartlett, clutching at his chest, collapse on to his knees and then very slowly fall face down in the dust. Behind him, also on her knees, was Heather. As Cobb slightly raised himself to look at her, she dropped the gun and began to, cry.

'Zac! You OK?' Neil ran up.

'What the hell is all this?' A voice demanded and all three stopped what they were doing to look up at the furious marshal, his bewildered deputy behind him. 'Mind telling me!'

Marshal Hepworth scratched his head. 'This is way, way beyond me.' He had already sent Tommy out to the Circle B to determine the situation out there. Bartlett's body lay at the undertakers. The excitement had died down and Glory had almost returned to normal.

'Do you believe me?' Heather asked.

'Yeah, of course I do.'

'And Miss Watkins can go free?'

'She's done nothing wrong. But, Heather, when the judge arrives he'll probably want you to make a statement.'

Heather nodded. That was a small price to pay.

The marshal turned to look at Neil. He hadn't taken much notice of him, a stranger to the town, so far. 'And who's this?'

After a heartbeat of tense quiet, Cobb said, 'He's someone who helped us. He saved our lives.'

'Oh?' Hepworth looked harder at Neil. 'He's not the stagecoach robber Bill and Dolly told me about?'

There was another tense moment.

'No,' Cobb said. He heard Neil let out an indrawn breath while he stared at Hepworth, daring the man to call him a liar.

Hepworth didn't bother. He was town marshal, and only concerned with what happened in the town. Stagecoach robberies were the jurisdiction of the county sheriff. By the time the county sheriff got round to looking for the robbers both Cobb and this young man would be long gone.

'I guess you'll be leaving soon?' he said, just to give them both the hint.

'As soon as possible.' Cobb just hoped that nothing would prevent his departure this time.

Outside Heather flung her arms round him. 'Zac, thank you for not giving Neil away!'

'Yeah, thanks, Mr Cobb.'

'God knows what Mr Bellington would say.'

'Mr Bellington won't know.'

Cobb kissed the girl lightly. 'No, I guess he won't at that. What are you going to do now, Heather?'

'Well, first of all I'm going home and have a good long bath and change out of these filthy clothes. Then I'm going to have a drink and treat myself to an enormous meal in the hotel restaurant.'

Cobb wondered about asking if he could share any or all of these things with the girl, especially the bath. He decided against it. What had happened between the two of them out at the Circle B belonged in the past. It was best just to say goodbye. They'd never meet again.

'After that,' she shrugged, 'I don't really know. There's nothing and no one to keep me in Glory. Perhaps I will go to San Francisco. I've always wanted to and there I can make a fresh start.' She gave Cobb a long hug. 'Thank you, for everything.'

After Cobb had seen Heather home, Neil trailing along not knowing what else to do, Cobb said, 'We'll go to the doctor in a while but how about a drink first? I could sure do with one.'

'Er, yeah, all right.' Neil sounded a bit dubious, as if he couldn't really believe that a lawman was offering to drink with him; as if now that Heather was no longer there he thought it was some sort of trick and that Cobb would hand him over to the law after all.

'Come on then.'

It was almost dark by the time they got to the saloon. As they neared its doors, a figure stepped out of the nearby alley and confronted them.

'Been waiting for you.'

It was Gary Travis.

'So this is where you've gotten to kid. Wondered. Thought you'd be in jail. What you doing with him? He's the lawman ain't he?'

'It's a long story.'

'Well, are you coming with me now?' Travis spoke belligerently. 'Or what?'

Cobb felt, rather than saw Neil glance at him. 'Look, Travis, I don't want any trouble. What you and your brother do is no concern of mine.'

'That's good,' Travis sneered.

'But it seems to me that you're the one leading him into bad ways and without you he might stand a chance of leading a normal life.'

'Really?'

'Yes, really. Neil,' Cobb caught hold of Neil's arm, 'you don't have to go with your brother if you don't want to.'

'Where the hell else can he go? Jail? He'd want to do that I'm damn sure.'

'He can stay with me.' Cobb was aware of Neil's startled look, as if he couldn't believe what he had heard. Cobb himself couldn't quite believe what he'd said.

'What do you want him for? He's goddamned useless.'

'I need a helper.'

'So do I. And he's my kin.'

'Don't seem you worried much about him when he was caught robbing the stage. I seem to remember you rode off and left him.'

'I was keeping an eye on you all.'

'Oh yes? So where have you been? Why didn't you try to rescue him?'

'Perhaps we ought ta hear who the kid wants to go with. Come on, Neil, tell this goddamned lawman what to do with hisself. Then come with me, the brother who's always looked after your best interests, and who loves you and wants to do best by you.'

Neil stared at them both. It didn't take him long to make up his mind. 'I'll stay with Mr Cobb,' he said.

'You little bastard!' Travis snarled and his hand went towards his gun.

Cobb was much quicker. His hand snaked down and the gun was out and pointing at Travis before Gary had pulled his gun halfway from the holster. The man came to a wide-eyed halt.

'Be a good loser, Travis. Your brother has made his choice.'

'You ain't heard the last of this, neither of you.' But Travis knew when he was beaten and it was an empty threat. He slunk away and disappeared into the shadows.

'Do we have anything to fear from him?'

'No, he ain't a backshooter, Zac.' Neil grimaced at the look Cobb gave him. It was obviously one thing for Heather to use the man's Christian name and quite another for him to get so informal. 'Er, Mr Cobb that is, er, did you mean what you said? Can I stay with you?'

Cobb hadn't meant it, not when he'd spoken. He'd said it on the spur of the moment. He liked to work alone. He didn't want anyone to help him. A helper would only get in his way, especially an idiot like Neil who didn't have the sense he was born with, who he'd have to look out for.

Now he heard the hopeful note in the young man's voice. If he said no, Neil would return to a life of crime. And somewhere along the way he'd end up getting caught or shot or lynched, probably before long too. Neil might not be the brightest of people but he deserved better than that. However much Cobb might come to regret it, what else could he do but stand by what he'd said?

'Yes, I did, we'll give it a try.'

'Thanks, Mr Cobb, I won't let you down.'

'Better not.'

Cobb groaned inwardly. A private detective riding with an outlaw! Christ knew what Mr Bellington would have to say about that!

The publishers hope that this book has given you enjoyable reading. Large Print Books are especially designed to be as easy to see and hold as possible. If you wish a complete list of our books, please ask at your local library or write directly to: Dales Large Print Books, Long Preston, North Yorkshire, BD23 4ND, England.

This Large Print Book for the Partially sighted, who cannot read normal print, is published under the auspices of

THE ULVERSCROFT FOUNDATION

Other DALES Western Titles In Large Print

ELLIOT CONWAY
The Dude

JOHN KILGORE
Man From Cherokee Strip

J. T. EDSON
Buffalo Are Coming

ELLIOT LONG
Savage Land

HAL MORGAN
The Ghost Of Windy Ridge

NELSON NYE
Saddle Bow Slim